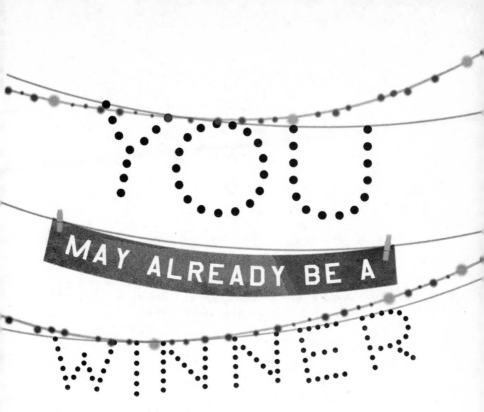

YOU

MAY ALREADY BE A

WINNER

ANN DEE ELLIS

DIAL BOOKS FOR YOUNG READERS

DIAL BOOKS FOR YOUNG READERS
An imprint of Penguin Random House LLC
375 Hudson Street
New York, NY 10014

Printed in the United States of America

Library of Congress Cataloging-in-Publication Data

Names: Ellis, Ann Dee, author.
Title: You may already be a winner / Ann Dee Ellis.
Description: New York, NY : Dial Books for Young Readers, [2017] |
Summary:
Twelve-year-old Olivia endeavors to care for her younger sister, possibly
make a new friend in the quirky and secretive Bart, and keep hope alive
for her, her family, and her community of idiosyncratic neighbors at Sunny
Pines Trailer Park.
Identifiers: LCCN 2016032501 | ISBN 9781101993859 (hardcover)
Subjects: | CYAC: Parent and child—Fiction. | Sisters—Fiction. | Trailer
camps—Fiction.
Classification: LCC PZ7.E4582 Yo 2017 | DDC [Fic]—dc23 LC record
available at https://lccn.loc.gov/2016032501

1 3 5 7 9 10 8 6 4 2

Design by Mina Chung • Text set in ITC Esprit

To my brave Milo, full of light, heart,
and imagination

CHAPTER 1

One day I sunk to the bottom of the pool and died.

People were screaming and a boy named Troy jumped in and even though he was a lifeguard and he had a whistle, he was scared.

Very very scared.

He jumped in and I saw him coming and I said, "Too late. I'm already dead." And he said, nothing. Because he was lugging my body to the surface.

People screamed. Especially Mom.

She was saying: "NO! NO! NO! MY BABY!"

And someone was holding her back because she was trying to jump in with me and Troy, but this would only complicate things.

Troy tried tried tried to get me over to the side of the pool and there was a crowd, including my old best friend Carlene and her new best friend Bonnie. They were bawling and the other lifeguards were yelling at Troy and he was saying, "I GOT IT!"

I was flopping around, turning blue, and now my mom was passed out.

When he finally got me to the deck, his lips were on my lips and he was breathing hard into my lungs. Though I'd never been kissed, my soft mouth molded to his as he tried to breathe life back into my body. During one of the intervals he was surprised to find himself no longer blowing breath into my mouth. But rather I was blowing breath into his.

"Olivia.

"Olivia.

"OLIVIA!"

I splashed up from the back float, the sound of the water and people and Mom.

She stood on the deck with her hand on her hip, her Naturalizer shoes, and her horrible Merry Maids uniform.

Everyone stared at her.

"What is wrong with you? Get your sister and get out. We're leaving."

A man with a snake tattoo on his neck gave me a sorry look and I gave him a none-of-your-business look, and Mom said, "Did you hear me?"

"Okay," I said.

"Where is she?" Mom said.

"She's right . . ."

I looked around. She was here. She was just here. Playing with a little boy in the shark shorts.

"Where is she, Olivia?"

"Hang on," I said.

The pirate ship was swarming with kids but no pink swimsuit.

My heart fluttered. I never lost her. Ever.

I swam to the side.

Nowhere.

The other side.

Panic now.

"Olivia," Mom said.

Then a lady in a bikini said to me, "She's over there."

At the corner of the pool stood my baby sister in her pigtails and chubby bum, talking to a man. A very big man with a big belly and a big beard, crouching down next to her.

Mom probably saw it at the same time because she let out a shriek.

And even though it was okay, even though his name was Kyle and he worked for the DMV and he was trying to help Berkeley find me, even though all those things, I got grounded for a week.

....

Dear Dad,

I have a boyfriend named Troy. He's a life-guard. I think you'd like him.

Mom thinks he's really nice and we might have him over for dinner. I wish you could meet him.

Love,
Liv

P.S. Mom grounded me for no reason.

....

CHAPTER 2

Today forty-six people in New Jersey won the lottery.

They were going to split a 324-million-dollar pot and they are so happy! One lady was homeless! One man was home from Afghanistan and now he doesn't have to go back! One person was already rich but now she's richer!

Mom said, "Olivia. Get off the computer and get your sister dressed."

I stared at the screen. Three hundred and twenty-four divided by forty-six was around seven million. What if I won seven million? Mom could quit her job and I could buy my own phone and Berkeley could have all the Beanie Babies she wanted and we could live in a real house.

Maybe even Dad would come back.

Maybe all we needed was seven million dollars.

"Olivia. Do you hear my voice?" she said.

I looked at her. "What?"

"Get your sister dressed."

Today I was going to enter at least ten contests. That was my goal. I always enter the HGTV Dream House

Giveaway and the Publishers Clearing House and then a few more regulars. But today I was going to find better ones. New ones.

My favorite part of entering was when the contest said this one thing: *You May Already Be a Winner*. It made me think that somewhere, probably somewhere fancy like New York City or Paris, someone was holding a big old suitcase of cash with my name all typed in gold. Or maybe on a tropical island where it never snowed and where the air smelled like coconuts was a house that was made especially for me, decorated in green and purple, my favorite colors. Or even there could be a lifetime supply of Twix bars just waiting in the UPS truck.

"Olivia," Mom said again.

"Okay," I said.

Mom's sister, Susan, who has money and lives in Wisconsin and who I have only seen twice, sent us the computer. It is my best thing. The only person who maybe loved it more than me was Dad who spent so many hours on it at night that he and Mom would get in fights.

But he's gone.

"Now!" Mom said, and I turned it off.

Berkeley was watching *Sesame Street* and coughing.

"Berk. Cover your mouth," Mom said. She grabbed her keys and her Diet Coke and she said to me, "Maybe you should stay home again. The day care is being jerks about the cough."

"Okay," I said.

Every morning Mom did this.

She would say Berk isn't going to day care because of a cough, or because Berkeley had a long night, or because Mom was running late, but really, Berkeley hadn't been to day care for weeks and I hadn't been to school in just as long.

Then she said, "But both of you need to get dressed. We're not barbarians."

I nodded.

"No computer. And turn out all the lights. The electricity bill was insane last month and no library."

"Okay," I said.

We used to hang out at the library.

Then they asked why we weren't in school.

So we can't go anymore.

Mom went out the door and she got in the Pontiac and I yelled, "Mom."

And she says, "What?"

And I say, "Does Utah have a lottery?"

And she rolled her eyes and shut the car door. Roared down the road and almost hit the SLOW DOWN sign.

~

Ten minutes later I watched Carlene and her cousin Lala walk to school.

I don't walk to school with Carlene anymore, which means I don't eat lunch with her, which also means I don't really know what's going on, like who likes who or who wore what or who got suspended or who is cool and who isn't.

Also, now I'm not Carlene's best friend anymore.

....

Dear Dad,

Hey! There is a new restaurant that everyone is talking about. It is called WaffleLove. They have waffles there. I have never had one yet because I'm waiting for you. Do you think you'll come? They are five dollars each but you can get all kinds of toppings. Carlene told me about it. She's had sixteen of them since they opened.

The Carters are gone but their trampoline is still there. The dad got arrested by the cops and then Tammy and the kids moved out in the middle of the night but they left the tramp! So Berk and I sort of took it over. I can do a front flip.

Love, Olivia

P.S. How long are you going to be gone?

....

CHAPTER 3

My dad is thirty.

My mom is thirty.

I am twelve but pretty much almost thirteen.

Thirty Thirty Thirteen. 30 30 13.

First I drew the numbers.

Then I colored them.

Then I showed them to Berk. I said, "Look: Thirty Thirty Thirteen."

She glanced over from her dolls.

She said, "So?"

"It's a lucky year," I said.

"What do you mean?" she asked.

I told her how the number three is perfect because it's like a triangle—a number for each corner and how me and Mom and Dad would all have threes in our ages this year. And how Mom and Dad had me when they were seventeen and seventeen minus three is fourteen and we lived at 14 Sunny Pines Lane and in six months I would be turning thirteen and six divided by two is three.

She stared at me. "So?"

"So do you see all the threes? It's lucky," I said.

"Luck isn't real," she said, playing with her dolls again.

Luck isn't real. Dad used to say this. Luck isn't real. You make your own lot in life.

But he was wrong and Berk was wrong.

"Berkeley," I said, "look at me."

She glanced over. "What?"

"Luck is real."

She shrugged.

Luck IS real.

I entered *fifteen* contests that day.

CHAPTER 4

Every morning after Mom leaves I do these things:

Enter at least ten contests but usually way more

Make my bed and make Berkeley make hers

Put away the dishes from last night

Exercise

Fifteen push-ups. The boy ones.

Thirty sit-ups and I make sure to keep my lower back on the floor, because Jillian Michaels says that if you don't have good form, don't do it at all.

I once entered her personal training sweepstakes. She sends me emails and texts every day even though I don't have a phone so I put in a fake phone number. Maybe someone in Texas or somewhere is getting fitness texts from Jillian Michaels.

Twenty-five squats and twelve lunges on each leg.

Berkeley watches from the couch and lets me know if I have bad form.

She says, "You aren't doing them right."

And so then I do them lower.

Then I do plank. I've gone two minutes and thirty-eight seconds.

After I exercise we go outside. We always try to make it out there by nine thirty because that's when Delilah gets her lunch hour from her early morning shift at Shirley's Bakery. Delilah is old like a grandma and has big round cheeks and bright red hair and a roly-poly body. She likes to hug you so warm, it feels better than a fleece blanket.

She lives alone at the opposite corner of the trailer park from us.

Sometimes Mom goes over there and she and Delilah watch shows together. Sometimes we go over, too. My favorites to watch are *Iron Chef* and *Fixer Upper*.

So every morning we try to get out there by the time Delilah comes home because if we're lucky, she brings us the leftover cinnamon rolls or raspberry danishes or one time she brought us an entire loaf of pull-apart orange bread that me and Berk ate so fast, I had to lie down afterward.

"Go easy," Delilah always says, because she's seen me and Berkeley eat.

And we always say, "We will."

And then she says, "Wake me up if you need anything."

And we say, "We will."

And then she winks and drives on down to her trailer and goes to sleep for an hour before she heads back to the bakery.

Then me and Berk, we go out to the trampoline and

start school. I use books from the library and I make Berkeley take the workbooks Mom gets for her at garage sales. Berkeley's ahead for her age. She missed the kindergarten deadline by four days and can already read chapter books. Dad always said she was smarter than him.

So we both read and do workbooks.
Then we have art.
I found lots of ideas on Pinterest:
Chalk animals
Chalk body outlines
Chalk outline of shadows
Chalk hopscotch
Painting on paper
Painting rocks
Painting fabric (only if it's already stained)
Coloring by number
Coloring in coloring books
Coloring pictures for Dad
Hearts
Cornstarch and water

Art is Berkeley's favorite time of day.
Then we eat lunch.
Then we take a nap on the tramp for quiet time.
Then we go for a walk and see if Randy, who is in

charge of the neighborhood, is in his trailer. Sometimes he'll pay us to pick up litter and then we can go buy candy at the pharmacy down the road. If he's not around, we sometimes spy on Melody, who is married to a man named Harry.

Melody has long blond hair and big blue eyes and lots and lots of lipstick and she's so sophisticated she doesn't belong here.

Neither does Harry, who wasn't so good looking but he was tall and wore ironed shirts.

But they lived here anyway and put up Christmas lights in July and had parties with people in tight jeans, and they are happy, except sometimes they scream at each other in the middle of the night and Harry leaves for a few weeks but he always comes back.

Melody will sit on her front steps when that happens and I think I should go talk to her but I don't.

Nobody does really.

So sometimes we spy on Melody because she likes to dance in her living room to music turned up loud. Or sit in her room, where the walls are covered with fancy posters of models and rock stars and cats.

If neither of them were around, we might walk to the river and watch the fish for science.

Or sometimes we look for money with Dad's old metal detector.

Then school gets out for the normal people and I watch Carlene come home and she sometimes says hey and I say hey, and then instead of coming over and seeing how I'm doing or when do I think I'll go back to school or seeing if I want to go to her house and watch YouTube videos, instead of any of that, she just goes inside. Berkeley plays with her friends, which she has two of, Sadie and Jane Johnson, who are twins that stay with their grandparents after school till their parents get off work. Sadie and Jane are in kindergarten but they can't read so Berkeley pretends like she's their teacher, which she is.

And then I sit.

And then the day is almost over.

And then I make macaroni or spaghetti or potatoes.

And then I check my email to see if I've won anything— one time I got a whole box of Kool-Aid packets, another time I got a free subscription to *Modern Dog Magazine*, and even another time I won a grandfather clock which we never got because I had to pay shipping and handling.

And then Mom gets home.

And then we eat.

And then we watch *Wheel of Fortune*.

And then we go to sleep.

CHAPTER 5

We live in a trailer park attached to a KOA, which stands for KAMPGROUNDS OF AMERICA. One side is for people who are driving across the country and who wouldn't spend more than one or two nights if they could help it, and on the other side there's a baseball field for middle-aged people who played softball games until late at night, yelling things like "Hey, Fatty! Hit the ball!"

Going through all of that there's a river and a running and biking trail that leads clear to the lake.

Anyway, this means all the time, all day all night, whether campers over at the KOA, spectators at the softball games, or joggers in spandex and hats, there are people watching us.

Watching us sit on the tramp.

Watching us eat pineapple on the roof.

Watching us lay in the kiddie pool.

It also means that we get to watch them right back.

We watch the softball games and find quarters under the bleachers.

We throw pebbles at the campers and eat their left-over chips.

And most of all, we make fun of the people who exercise on the river trail.

Dad and I would play this game we called "Guess Who's Coming," which is where we would sit on the front porch and watch the running trail. We'd make guesses who was going to come around the bend next. We'd give them a name and an occupation and see if it fit.

Dad was always the best at it.

He'd say, "The next guy that comes is going to be Earl, a businessman by day, candymaker by night."

"Candymaker?"

"Sure," he'd say. "A famous one. Known for his caramel lollipops with Argentinian ant legs inside."

I'd laugh and then, some man with skinny arms and a bald head in tiny shorts would show up. He for sure was a businessman, but you could also see how he could have an exotic sweet business on the side.

Or Wanda, a deep-sea diver who lives in Utah because she is scared of water.

"What?"

"Long story," Dad would say, and then, just like that, a lady would come around the corner wearing all black spandex from head to toe. Even with a tight skullcap.

Amazing.

Now that he was gone, I tried to get Berk to do it with me.

She didn't really get it and usually it was just teenage jerks, who we don't look at because they yell at us and say dirty things.

But still.

A lot of people come on that trail. Some you expect and some you don't.

One day we were sitting on the tramp, me working on figuring out what x means in $2x-8=4$ from my textbook and Berk coloring Aurora, and on that day, we heard something.

Usually you don't hear anything that much because the river's too loud.

This time, though, whoever it was, he was louder than the river.

He was yelling something. Or singing something.

About burning down a house.

Berkeley looked at me. I looked at her.

Then we both watched to see who it was.

"A crazy man named Ted who flies airplanes and wins hot-dog-eating contests," I whispered to Berk.

"What?" she said, but then he came into view.

A regular-sized boy, brown hair, white sweatband around his head, normal face except for lots of freckles, yellow tank top that said "I hate cats," and baggy jeans.

He was also sweating and sort of jogging, if you could call it that, and, like I said, singing.

Loud.

I couldn't help myself, I laughed.

Berkeley laughed, too.

When he got to the break in the chain-link fence where you could come into the trailer park rather than keep going on the trail and where there's a bench, he sat down.

He was breathing hard, his chest going up and down, gulping for air, and even though we were ten feet away, he hadn't seen us yet.

He kept singing to himself. *People on their way to work said, Baby what did you expect. Gonna burst into flame, go ahead.*

He had a bad voice, I'm sad to say, and he had to be about my age. Twelve or thirteen.

He looked at his watch.

Then he looked over at the trailer park.

Berkeley whispered to me, "Who is he?"

I shrugged and put a finger to my lips to keep quiet.

He stood up.

Pulled out a piece of paper from his pocket.

He studied the paper for a bit and then came right through the gate. He didn't look our way and I was glad.

It wasn't often people who didn't live here went through the gate and in my opinion it was quite suspicious.

Suddenly he turned and said, "Olivia?"

And I said, "Who? Me?"

And he said, "Olivia Hales, right?"

And I said, "Uh. Yes."

And he said, "It's me."

And I said, "Who?"

And he said, "Me."

And I said, "Who are you?"

And he smiled, his face bright. Then he said, "I'm from the lottery. You've won three hundred and twenty-four million dollars."

And my heart beat like a tambourine and Berkeley said, "What does it mean?"

And he said, "It means you and your sister are going to be very happy." Then he took out a camera from his baggy jeans and he said, "What do you want to say to the world, now that you're rich and famous?"

And I was overcome with emotion, tears pouring out of my eyes, and all I could say was, "Thank you. Thank you. Thank you."

And then, because he couldn't help it, he took me into his arms and we began to kiss.

"Olivia?"

I blinked a few times.

"Olivia?"

It was Berkeley.

"What?"

"You were doing it again," she said.

"Doing what?"

"Doing that thing."

"I don't know what you're talking about," I said.

And we were going to get in an argument but then I remembered.

"Where is he?"

She pointed to the boy who was now across the way, looking in the windows of some of the trailers.

Which was definitely not allowed.

CHAPTER 6

When you drive into Sunny Pines Trailer Park there is a
sign that says:

NO TRESPASSING.

There's also a sign that says:

PRIVATE PROPERTY.

And then the:

SALE! DOLLS AND COLLECTIBLES that Mrs. Sydney
Gunnerson puts out just about every week because she
is fancy and she collects fancy things like teacups and
wigs and cookie jars and glass dolls that are hand painted.

"Do you paint them?" Berkeley asked one time, and
Sydney, who used to be in the opera in New York but
works at Walmart now and Sundays plays her music so
loud you can barely hear the rap music from the Conways' trailer, Sydney said, "My dear, these little ones are
painted in Italy." And then she showed us the bottom of
a blond doll's foot and it said: *Hand Painted in Italy.*

She doesn't get much business because the dolls
are over thirty dollars and the other things are expensive, too. But she sits out there every Saturday, all the
same, an umbrella over her head, rain or shine.

Sometimes we sit by her and yell at cars to get their attention for her sale.

She says to only do it to nice cars like Cadillacs and Subarus. "Avoid the minivans," she says.

There's also a ONE WAY sign for the road.

A sign that said NO SOLICITORS.

A SLOW DOWN sign.

And then finally, one that said NO PEEPING TOMS.

This was because of another problem that came up at the Home Owners Association meeting that I wasn't allowed to go to.

Was this kid looking in trailers a case of a Peeping Tom? I wasn't completely sure what a Peeping Tom was now that I thought about it. I'd have to Google it.

In any case, he was not supposed to be doing what he was doing.

Berkeley said, "What is he looking for?"

And I said, "I don't know but he's breaking the law."

And she said nothing.

Instead she yelled, "DO YOU KNOW YOU'RE BREAK-ING THE LAW?"

I gasped.

Berkeley was a five-year-old but she was always doing things I would never dare do: Talk to people. Yell things. Eat mushrooms.

He turned to look at us.

I lay down on the tramp on top of a bunch of papers and pretended like I was asleep.

The kid said, "What?" Like he didn't hear, which was crazy because Berkeley was loud.

And then Berk just went ahead and did it again. "YOU ARE BREAKING THE LAW."

I wanted to grab her. Tell her to stop. But I also didn't want him to think I was awake if I could help it.

I heard him walk over.

I held still.

"I'm not breaking the law."

"Yes you are," Berkeley said.

"No, I'm not."

"Yes, you are, huh Olivia?"

I didn't move.

"Olivia?"

Still lay there. Tried to send energy. Act like I'm asleep. Act like I'm asleep. Tell him I'm asleep.

"Olivia?" she said again.

"Is she dead?" he asked.

"No."

"She looks dead."

"No," Berkeley said, but I could hear she was getting nervous, which was so stupid.

"I'm not dead," I said, my eyes still closed.

They were quiet.

Then he said, "What are you doing?"

"I'm resting."

"You're resting."

"Yes. I'm resting." I opened one eye. "Can't a person rest?"

"Yes," he said. "Yes, they can."

Then he did this: He got on the tramp and lay down right next to me; he was practically on top of my pre-algebra book.

Just like that.

I said, "What are you doing?"

And he said, "I'm resting."

And that's how I met a boy.

CHAPTER 7

Bart sat with us on the tramp for four hours and thirty-three minutes.

He even said that, he said, "I've been here four hours and thirty-three minutes," and I said, "How do you know?"

He showed me his watch which had a stopwatch and he said, "I time everything."

"You time everything?"

"Everything. Time is very important to me," he said.

"Me too," I said, and it was true. Maybe I didn't use a stopwatch but my calendar and my wristwatch that Mom gave me were things I had to have. They were the way I could know what was going to happen next and when the online contests ended and when the library was safe to go to and when Mom was getting home and mostly they were my only way to know how much time had passed.

Time could go slow and you could get so bored checking the clock you wonder if it's broken. Sometimes just waiting for water to boil for hot dogs or macaroni or ramen felt like it took forever and everyone was dying of hunger, including yourself, and it still wouldn't boil.

On the other hand, time could also trick you and speed along so fast, you could forget to even get dinner going or you could miss out on getting doughnuts from Delilah or you could suddenly realize that your dad had been gone for almost a year.

"You're a time geek, too," he said, studying me, which made me feel weird but also who cares. And then he said this, he said, "I like you."

Just like that.

I tried not to but I smiled.

He told us his name was Bart.

"I'm Bart," he said.

And I thought Bart was not the best name but I didn't say so.

Berkeley said, "Why are you here?"

And he said, "I'm exercising."

"You're exercising?" she said, and I laughed.

He looked at me. "What's so funny?"

"Nothing," I said.

Then he told how he was cardiovascularly very fit and that he was training to run a hundred-mile race.

"A hundred miles?" I said.

"Yep," he said. "It's called an ultramarathon."

I almost told him I was in Jillian Michaels fitness club and I was probably going to live in Micronesia or Papua

New Guinea but instead I said, "How do you train?"

"I run all day pretty much."

"You do?" Berkeley said.

"I do."

"You run all day?" she said.

"All day."

"Why aren't you running now?" she said.

"Because I'm sitting with you guys."

Why was he sitting with us? I thought. I tried not to look at him. To just stare straight at the sky and act like it was normal for a boy to be lying next to me on a trampoline.

"If you run all day, when do you go to school?" Berkeley asked.

"I don't," he said.

Now I did look at him.

"You don't?" I asked.

"Nope."

I don't know why but that made me feel happy. I said, "I don't either."

He smiled at me. "Then we're the same," he said.

"Yes," I said. "The same."

I thought I should ask why he didn't go to school.

I thought he should ask why I didn't go to school.

But neither of us did. Which felt even more perfect.

Then Berkeley said, "My sister does push-ups."

I felt myself get hot.

"You do?" he said.

"Sometimes," I said.

"She does every day," Berkeley said. And she was smiling. "She's strong."

He was still looking at me and I was back to looking at the sky.

He said, "On your knees?"

I said, "Knees?"

And he said, "The push-ups."

I laughed. "No way. I do real ones."

He said, "How many?"

I said, "As many as I want."

He said, "I challenge you."

And I said, "No thank you," even though I was burning now. What if I could beat him? What if I could?

He said, "Are you scared?"

And I said, "No."

And he said, "Then why not."

And I said, "Because I don't want to."

And he said nothing.

We just lay there and Berkeley sat there.

I was trying not to giggle and I don't even know why.

After a while Berkeley got bored. "Are we going to do our workbooks?" she asked.

And I said, "Why don't you do chalk?"

"Now?"

"Sure," I said.

She looked at Bart and then at me. "What about lunch?"

"It's not lunchtime," I said.

She stared for a bit and then she said, "Okay," and climbed off the tramp and got the sidewalk chalk.

Bart and I were sort of alone then.

We lay for a while.

Then he said, "Do you know who Steve Fossett is?"

Steve Fossett. Steve Fossett. Steve Fossett.

I tried to think about my history books. My science books. Was he from sports?

I wanted to know so badly.

But I didn't. So I said, "No. I don't know who he is."

And he said, "You should."

Ugh. Ugh. Ugh. I swallowed and said, "Why?"

He said, "He's only the greatest man who ever lived."

And I said, "Who is he?"

And he said, "I'll tell you later."

Which made me mad but I didn't say that.

Instead we talked about TV and how it was a total waste of time in his mind and also addictive and ruins lives. I said TV is not addicting and I said it wasn't that bad for example on the History Channel you could learn about Robert Peary, who discovered the North Pole, and you could learn about how the five-second rule is not true, you can get all kinds of bacteria and fungus on your hot dog if it's on the floor for a millisecond, and he said no way.

And I said yes way.

And he said he ate tons of stuff that had been on the floor for hours.

I said gross.

"And besides," he said, "you could find that out by the internet, not TV."

"I found it out on TV."

"So."

"So, TV is good."

He sighed. Then he said he knew a guy who spent his entire life in front of the TV and his family was like, come to the park, and he was, like, no I have to watch a rerun of *Lost*. And they were, like, have Christmas with us, and he was, like, no, I have to see if blah blah does blah blah. He even had a toilet installed in the couch.

"What are you talking about?"

"He had a couch where the middle cushion had a hole in it for the toilet."

"You're lying," I said.

"I'm not," he said.

I said, "Oh."

Then he told me that it was a myth that people couldn't drink a whole gallon of milk at one sitting. I said, "No one can do that." And he said, "Someone could, if it was skim for sure."

He said next time he came over he'd show me.

Next time is what he said.

He smelled like bananas. And sweat. And his arm was touching mine. And he said *next time* he was going to drink a gallon of skim milk.

My heart was pounding out of my chest. I had no idea what was happening but I hoped it was never going to stop.

Next, he told a story about a creepy man who sat in his front window and waved at people all day.

"That seems nice not creepy," I said.

"Really? You don't think it's weird to spend your whole day staring out the window watching people?"

I felt a little stupid then because mostly all Berk and I did was watch people.

At lunch we ate tuna fish sandwiches, which I made with Doritos sticking out which is my private recipe, and soft batch cookies that Mom bought at Big Lots and that we were supposed to save for Sunday dinner.

I brought out a plate of everything and was going to ask if he wanted some but he grabbed a sandwich before I could get a word out. He even said it was delicious, which it was.

After lunch he gave Berkeley a Jolly Rancher and she

said, "What's this?" and he said, "It's for you," and she said, "I can't have hard candy," and he said, "Sure you can."

Berkeley looked at me. My mom tried to be strict about suckers and things because we didn't have a dentist.

Normally I would've said don't eat it. I might've even taken it from her and thrown it away, but for some reason I felt a little different.

So I said, "It's up to you."

And she said, "Really?"

And I said, "Yep."

And so she ate it.

From then on, Berkeley loved Bart.

She kept asking him things like, "Do you like princesses?"

And he kept saying things like, "No."

And she said, "What about mermaids?"

And no. He did not like mermaids.

Did he like hair?

He did like hair but only certain types of hair.

She asked what kind of hair.

He said, "I like curly hair," and I swear to you he glanced at my hair which is so curly you can't even straighten it with an iron and I tried not to notice. "And long hair. And Mohawks."

I thought this was funny because his hair was straight and short.

She said, "What's a Mohawk?"

And he said, "You know what a Mohawk is."

And she said, "No I don't."

And he acted very upset and I tried not to laugh. He said, "Berkeley, right?"

And she said, "Yes," and he said, "A Mohawk is probably the best hairdo you can ever have."

She said, "It is?"

And he said, "Yes."

And she said, "Do princesses have them?"

And he said, "Cool ones do."

They talked like that for a long time, which I thought was weird but also nice. Sometimes we talked to a lot of people in the neighborhood. Other times, especially if Delilah was out of town, we could go days without anyone talking to us. Even Mom was too tired to talk.

So he was nice.

And weird.

But nice.

As the sun lowered in the sky and everyone was getting home and yelling and throwing footballs and softball practice plus more joggers, he said, "I better go."

He stood up, the tramp gently bouncing. And I realized I hadn't asked him the two most important questions I'd been waiting to ask and soon he was going to be gone.

"Wait," I said as he jumped off the tramp.

He turned and looked at me.

I said my number one: "Why were you looking in that trailer?"

He said, "What trailer?"

I said, "That trailer," and I pointed across the road.

He acted like he didn't know what I was talking about.

"We saw you looking."

"Oh that," he said. "I would tell you but then I'd have to kill you."

"What?" I said.

Then he said, "FBI stuff."

"Huh?"

Then he said, "I have to go."

FBI stuff? What was he talking about? But he was getting ready to go so then I asked him the second question, which was much worse than the first. I said, "Are you coming back?" I felt dumb immediately.

He smiled. "Yes. I'll bring milk."

He had a lot of freckles and bright blue eyes and a dimple.

He reminded me of a boy in a movie. I didn't know what movie or anything, but just someone who would be in a movie. Someone interesting. Someone different.

He said, "See ya." And I said, "See ya." And Berk said, "See ya."

And he was gone.

....

Dear Dad,

I have a new friend. His name is Bart and
he's going to run a hundred miles in a race.
He also knows a lot about a lot of different
things. I think you'd like him. Also, he makes
my heart hurt. Please disregard that I just said
that unless you have something you could tell
me that would be advice.

How are the hoodoo rock formations? I put
up a map and some pictures of Bryce Canyon
on my wall.

Maybe I could come visit this summer. Maybe
I could bring Bart. I think you'd like him.

Love,
Olivia

P.S. Did you know you can drink a gallon of
milk in an hour? Especially if it's skim.

....

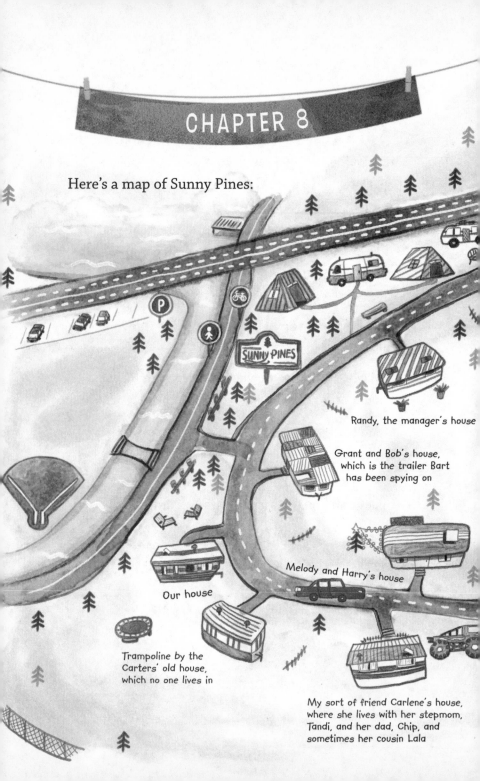

CHAPTER 8

Here's a map of Sunny Pines:

SUNNY PINES

Randy, the manager's house

Grant and Bob's house,
which is the trailer Bart
has been spying on

Melody and Harry's house

Our house

Trampoline by the
Carters' old house,
which no one lives in

My sort of friend Carlene's house,
where she lives with her stepmom,
Tandi, and her dad, Chip, and
sometimes her cousin Lala

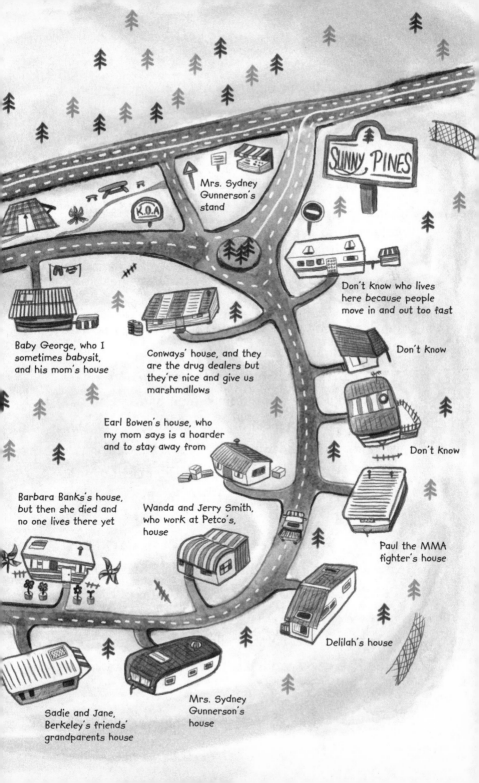

Why would he spy on Grant and Bob?

Grant and Bob are twins.

Bob got married and then got divorced and his ex-wife is named Heaven and sometimes she comes over and brings him meat loaf which I know because one time she left it on the porch when he wasn't home and Delilah's poodle got into it and Bob happened to pull up in his truck right when the dog was wolfing it down and he started yelling, "You stupid dog. Get away from my meat loaf."

I was watching from my window and I saw the whole thing. He yelled that and then he kicked the dog so hard it made my stomach turn.

And that was right when Delilah came out looking for the dog and so there was a huge fight and Delilah was crying and Chip came out and was getting Bob to calm down and once he did calm down he said he was sorry.

"I'm sorry," he was telling Chip. He looked over at Delilah, who was sobbing on a bench holding the dog. "I am sorry. But I hardly ever get my meat loaf."

And Delilah yelled, her face a red balloon. "YOU CAN GET MEAT LOAF ANY OLD TIME BUT CAN YOU GET A PRECIOUS RUTHANNE? CAN YOU REPLACE A RUTHANNE?"

Ruthanne is Delilah's poodle, which she loves very much. I had never in my life ever heard Delilah yell at anyone.

And Bob said, "You can't get *this* meat loaf any old place. This is the best meat loaf in the state."

And I knew it was the one from his ex, Heaven.

So Bob lived there, and he was the mean one, and so did Grant who was his brother who never got married and was more of the dopey one. Both of them own three electronics shops and are super rich.

Dad told us so. "Those two are filthy rich," he said once.

But I didn't think they'd be rich because Grant wore horrible stretched-out T-shirts with big old sweat rings and jeans with holes all the time, and Bob wore these tight golf shirts that showed his fat rolls and sometimes he wore a tie with the shirt which looked really weird.

And one time Grant fell asleep while he was under his truck trying to fix it and Bob thought he'd been murdered so he called the cops and there was a search party organized because everyone in the park, even if they hate each other sometimes, they also love each other.

And me and Mom, we put Berkeley to bed and Dad stayed home, and then the two of us walked along the river trail with a flashlight looking for dead bodies.

Grant's dead body.

We held hands and she said, "If you see anything, squeeze my hand."

"Why can't I just tell you?" I asked.

"Nah," she said. "I've heard sometimes when you see

a dead body it takes your breath away. You can't say a word."

I smiled. I liked that my mom would tell me things like that. That she treated me like an adult. She used to say all the time that I was her best friend.

I was glad she let me go look for dead bodies with her.

We didn't find a thing.

Nobody did.

And it was very sad.

Then the next day, when people were all out eating bagels provided by Bob as a thank-you for searching for his dead brother and saying how tragic it was; Sydney Gunnerson said he probably got drunk and fell into the river; and Randy, who was very close friends with Bob and Grant because they played poker sometimes, he was crying and saying he should have watched out for him better; and then Delilah said he probably was floating around all puffy in the lake right now. When everyone was out talking like that, Grant just rolled out from under the truck and walked right into his trailer and drank a beer.

We all watched him through the window.

Inside their house are posters of girls and lots of antlers and a life-size statue of Princess Leia.

That was Bob and Grant's trailer and that's who Bart was trying to see, which made no sense.

CHAPTER 9

The next day the sun came up just like normal except not like normal, because maybe Bart would be back.

One bad thing: The computer wouldn't work.

The night before I wanted to find out who Steve Fossett was and the screen kept freezing. Mom and I got in a fight because she didn't think it needed to be fixed.

"It does need to be fixed," I said, and I almost told her that four of my contests ended soon and we could win so much money and a trip to Cabo San Lucas and possibly a year's supply of L'Oréal LOCK IT Bold Control hairspray.

But I didn't.

Because she was not in the mood. I could tell.

She took off her work shirt, walking around in just her bra, banging cupboards and slamming plates on the table. I had forgotten to make dinner.

"The car needs to be fixed. The swamp cooler is broken still. It's going to get hotter than Hades here in a couple of months. We have holes in the screen door and I haven't paid the HOA fees for five months."

She pulled out old ham.

And a bowl of Cheerios.

"Eat," she said. Then she went back into her room.

So no internet.

But today was a new day.

Berk and I ate our breakfast. We said bye to Mom. I didn't get to enter any contests but I made a goal to walk to the library right when school got out if Bart wasn't here. Or maybe he could come with us.

I did my exercises as fast as I could and then we hurried outside.

And sat.

And sat.

And sat.

Delilah stopped by with some cinnamon rolls.

She asked us what we were up to this weekend and I said not much and she said we could come over and watch TV later because she got off early, and I said thanks but really I was wanting her to leave so we could wait for Bart.

"You okay?" she asked me.

"Sure," I said.

And she gave me a look like she thought something was wrong but nothing was wrong. "Come get me if you need me, you hear?"

"Okay," I said.

"Okay," Berk said.

And then she left.

We sat.

And ate the cinnamon rolls.

I saved one for him.

And sat.

And sat.

And sat.

Berk said, "Do you think he'll come?"

I said, "I hope."

She said, "Me too."

We waited.

And waited.

And waited.

And waited.

After a while, Berkeley said she was hungry and picked up the cinnamon roll.

"Hey," I said. "That's for him."

"But I'm hungry," she said again.

"It's for him," I said again, and she put it back down.

I looked at my watch. Noon already. And we hadn't done any of our books.

Or art.

I made more tuna fish with Doritos sandwiches again, cut up some apples.

We ate but made sure to leave a little, just in case, to go along with his cinnamon roll.

And we both watched the trail.

There were a lot of moms with strollers that day.

And one man with a big old mustache who said, "What you looking at?"

I whispered to Berkeley to ignore him and look away. But he kept staring at us and this was one reason I thought I should take martial arts but Mom said I couldn't, but I was maybe going to ask Paul from down the street to give me some tips one day.

Then the man went away.

And then there were more moms, which I preferred.

After a long time, Berkeley said, "Is he coming?"

"I don't know. I think so."

We sat.

And sat. She got out her dolls.

She played.

I sat.

After another hour or so she said, "I wish he'd come."

I said, "Me too."

And she said, "Maybe he's running."

I said, "He's probably running."

She said, "Could you run a hundred miles?"

I wasn't good at running.

"I don't think so," I told her.

She stared at me and said, "Maybe you could."

I smiled. Berkeley always thought I was better than I was.

"Maybe," I said.

"You should try," she said.

"I should," I said.

And then we sat.

She said, "You do push-ups."

I said, "I do."

"Real ones," she said.

"Yes," I said, "real ones."

Then we sat some more.

Finally, Delilah came out of her trailer and yelled over to us. "You girls want to come over? *Cupcake Wars* is on."

Berkeley stood up. "Come on," she said. We love *Cupcake Wars*. And so does Delilah.

I looked at the path. Where was he?

"You go ahead," I said to Berk. "I'll come later."

"Are you sure?"

I nodded and she said, "Come get me if he comes?"

"Okay."

She skipped off down to Delilah's and I kept sitting.

I waited for Bart to come all day long.

He didn't come.

CHAPTER 10

We waited the next day. He still didn't come.

I ran around the trailer park just to see if Berkeley was right and maybe I could run a hundred miles. Maybe me and Bart could run together. I was going to do it ten times but then after six I got a side ache.

We waited more days.

A whole week went like that and I thought maybe Bart wasn't running a one-hundred-mile race.

I thought maybe we'd never see him again.

Even though he said he'd be back.

Because that's what people say.

CHAPTER 11

You can win a cottage on Papua New Guinea.

I once read a romance novel about a girl named Gretchen who ate cheese, and her father was a pirate captain, and one day when they were sailing through the Magellan Strait, there was a squall and her ship wrecked on Micronesia, which is practically Papua New Guinea, and she met a man named Juan.

And Juan loved her.

And she loved Juan.

But her father said, "NO! NO, Gretchen! He's a heathen!" (I looked up heathen on Wikipedia once. It means: a person who does not belong to a widely held religion, which I don't get why it's so bad but that's what it means.) But Gretchen didn't listen to her father. She listened to her heart. And she and Juan ran away together on a sailboat and then they sunk and died.

Dead.

I cried and cried and cried when they held hands and slowly submerged into the sea. I want to die like that.

I entered the Papua New Guinea contest twenty-four times.

I wondered if Bart knew about Papua New Guinea.

CHAPTER 12

Sometimes at night, my mom cries.

Sounds that make my whole body sad.

Mostly I lie in bed and try to go back to sleep.

Other times, I crawl in with her and she says, "Livy," and I say, "Mommy," and she curls me up next to her. She smells always like Curve perfume she gets from Walgreens and also like garlic if she's been cleaning at the Nelsons' house.

She curls me up tight, right up to her chest and she says things.

She says, "Can we do it? Can we do it just us girls?"

And I say, "We can, Mom. We can."

Or she says: "You know I love you. I love you so much."

And I say: "I know."

Or she says, "We don't have any milk and I don't get paid for three more days," and I say, "We don't need any," and she says, "We don't?" and I say, "We can just eat toast."

And she always says, "You're my one, Livy. I could never do this without you."

And I say . . .

~

I say . . .

I say, "Me too."

And that's the truth.

Even if she's been different since he left. Even if things are not how they were. Even if she's gone all the time. My mom, she's the best person I know.

I tell her that. I tell her and then I can't help it, then I start to cry and she holds me tight and we can do it. We can do it just us girls.

CHAPTER 13

One day I was watching Berk playing with her friends and not waiting for Bart when Carlene came out of her trailer in flip-flops and her purse she got from Santa's secret shop at school one year, which I helped pick out, and I thought maybe she was going to the pharmacy to buy a *People* magazine but instead she walked on over to me.

Like it was normal.

Like she used to do all the time.

"Hey," she said.

"Hey," I said. Keeping it cool. "You want to sit down?"

She came up. Sat on the railing next to me.

"What ya doin'?" she asked.

I don't know why I was so nervous because who cares. But I kept shaking and my hands were sweating.

"Nothing," I said.

She nodded. "Me either. I'm so bored."

"Yeah," I said back.

Then she said, "Guess what?"

"What?"

"My dad got in the Monster Jam up at West Jordan."

I gasped. Her dad, Chip, has a really nice truck that

he's been working on for forever and my dad helped him all the time and even ended up doing the paint job, and he did a good job, I think. It's got green slime coming out of a leopard's mouth and says *Mama's Nightmare* on the side.

"He got in?" I really felt so excited.

She smiled. "It happened last night. He qualified and he did better than he's ever done."

"Oh my gosh," I said, laughing. "That's so cool."

It felt normal to be talking like this. Like everything was normal. I couldn't count the hours we sat around watching our dads work on that thing.

A car came by and it was Paul the MMA fighter who I still hadn't asked for martial arts moves and I said, "Watch out for cars," to Berk and them because Paul is a bad driver.

Then I said to Carlene, "Is he going to win?"

She picked at her fingernails, which were bright pink with snowflakes.

"Probably. And if he does, we're all going to Vegas. Even Lala."

Lala was Carlene's cousin who lived with her sometimes and sometimes didn't live with her. She has good hair.

I said, "Wow."

Carlene said, "I could maybe take you."

I almost choked on nothing. "Really?" I said, trying to keep my voice regular.

She shrugged. "Probably. My dad said it would be a huge party and we could invite anyone."

"Even me?" I said.

"Sure," she said.

I hoped she was serious. I hope hope hoped she was serious. I wondered if Tandi would say it was okay. Or if Mom would.

It used to be that sometimes I went with Carlene and her family places, before everything happened with Dad.

Chip could be nice. He always has sunflower seeds and he and my dad would go fishing. Or go to demolition derbys or work on their cars.

He did yell a lot, though.

And her stepmom, Tandi, used to be Mom's best friend. They both worked at Merry Maids and they would help each other finish jobs. She came over all the time and sat on our counter and drank Diet Coke with Mom and on the weekends they'd color everyone's hair. Once Tandi did mine blond and Dad, when he got home that night, he said I looked like a siren.

I laughed when he said that. "Like a siren?" I didn't even know what that was and I told him that.

"It's somebody who traps boys," Dad said. "Isn't that right, LeAnn?"

Mom didn't say anything but it seemed like maybe this was from another fight. Sometimes they had fights that lasted weeks and weeks.

"LeAnn," Dad said, "isn't that right?"

She brought over the Hot Pockets and Berk came and sat down and he said, "Did you hear me?" And Mom, she said, "I heard you."

And he said, "So why don't you answer me?"

She shook her head. "Can we just eat?"

Dad stared at her and we all sat there and he said, "Your mom's just mad because she couldn't trap anyone even if she wanted to."

Mom didn't look at him and I didn't either and Berkeley was too little.

Finally, he picked up a Hot Pocket and took a big old bite, so then we could eat, too.

No one talked the rest of the night and the next day she and Tandi dyed my hair back to brown and Tandi kept saying things to Mom like, "He's a jerk. You know that, right? You don't have to put up with it," and Mom kept saying, "Shhhhusssh." And I know it was because I was right there.

So anyway, our families were close. We sometimes, all of us, including Mom and Dad and Berk, would go camping up Rock Canyon or at the reservoir. And sometimes just I would go with Carlene's family on trips. We once even stayed in Carlene's grandma's RV for a week and went to Lagoon and I went on the Colossal roller coaster thirty-six times and Carlene and I slept on the bunk above the driver and ate Skittles all night long.

Then everything changed.

They always change.

Except right then, Carlene was saying maybe I could come to Las Vegas.

I took a breath, and said a small prayer, which I sometimes do. Then I said, "When is the Monster Jam?"

"Like August."

"Oh," I said. "That would be fun. What day in August?"

She shrugged. "The Monster Jam in West Jordan is in June."

"Oh," I said. What day what day what day.

Then Tandi yelled for her.

"I have to go." And she went inside.

That night I convinced Mom to stop at the library on the way to the store.

She didn't want to but I said, "It will take me five minutes."

So she said, "Fine."

I ran in. Got on a computer and found out.

West Jordan Monster Jam: June 24.

Las Vegas Monster Jam: August 3.

It only took five minutes but then, when I got in the car, I realized I'd forgotten to look up Steve Fossett, which ruined my mood but only a little.

....

Dear Dad,

I'm going to Las Vegas! Mom said it's a good idea and it's with Carlene's family because Chip might qualify for the regionals!!!!!! In the truck!!!!! I'm not sure where we're staying but probably in one of the nice casinos like the Paris or MGM Grand. I can see if they can get an extra room if you want to meet us there or maybe we could pick you up. I bet Chip would want to see you. And Tandi.

I looked it up in our map book and Bryce is only an hour away from the freeway we'll be driving. You could come to the exit or something. Or maybe they could drop me off at the exit and I could come with you for a little bit. Or we could follow them in your car.

What kind of car do you have now?

We still have the Pontiac.

Okay.

Or you could call Chip yourself. Do you want to call him or should I ask? Just let me know. I know you're busy so if you can't it's okay. It's in August. I'll let you know more soon.

Also, that boy Bart has died. He was eaten by a cougar.

I'm going to send this in the mail because the computer is broken. I'll just address it to Bryce National Park Ranger Station? I hope you get it.

Love,

Liv

P.S. Maybe they have an award for the best paint job on the truck and you'd get a medal or something!!!!!!!!

....

CHAPTER 14

The next time I saw Carlene I was hoping things would be like last time and we could talk more about the Monster Jam and maybe I could have Chip call Dad.

But instead she was with her new best friend Bonnie.

She got Bonnie when we started at middle school because you meet new people there from all over the city not just our dumb-bum neighborhood.

Bonnie doesn't really talk to me or live anywhere near us, according to her.

"We live on Pleasantview."

"Where's Pleasantview?" I asked.

They both looked at each other and started giggling.

I tried not to feel dumb because maybe it was funny.

Then I said, "It sounds nice. Pleasant view."

Bonnie rolled her eyes. "It doesn't even mean that—we don't have a view of anything. It's just a neighborhood. And we have an actual YARD at my house."

Carlene turned red.

"We have yards," I said, because we did. Each trailer had a square of grass or cement and some had back squares, too. And one trailer, in the corner where the

Carters used to live, it had enough space for the tramp, which was pretty big if you asked me.

"These are not yards, huh, Carlene," Bonnie said.

Carlene was now bright red.

I waited for her to say something. To say they *were* real yards. That Earl Bowen had a sign that said KEEP OUT OF YARD and how could you have that if you didn't have a yard? And how Barbara Banks, who is now dead but still, how she won best landscaping by the Home Owners Association because she grew hollyhocks and had pinwheels and gnomes all over the place. I waited for her to tell Bonnie that she didn't know what she was talking about.

I waited and waited and waited.

I waited so long I thought Bonnie's face would fall off but then, finally, after fifty-five years, finally all quiet, Carlene said, "Not real yards."

Not real yards?

She wouldn't look at me and I wouldn't look at me either if I were her.

I was about to get up my courage to say something. To say you both are wrong. And this is a fine place to live and shut your faces. I was about to say something like that but then Bonnie said, "So why did your dad leave?"

Just then a gigantic black mamba fell on Bonnie's head.

CHAPTER 15

She screamed.

Carlene screamed.

I said, "Don't move! Don't move!"

But Bonnie didn't listen. She was jumping up and down and throwing her arms all over the place and the big fat black mamba opened its big fat black mouth and bam, bit her right in the forehead.

This was very sad because black mambas are the most venomous snakes in the whole world. Native to Africa, this one was probably an illegal pet to the man with the buzz cut who moved into the pink trailer with the motorcycle who I haven't met yet. Most people don't realize that you're a goner if a mamba gets its teeth into you.

Bonnie fell to the ground.

Carlene was still screaming and though some would think I should have helped Bonnie, I knew better. Her face was already bloating and she was turning purple. She was a goner. RIP.

So instead of Bonnie, I jumped for the snake, barely grabbing his tail before it slithered off into the bushes and had babies and infested the entire neighborhood.

We wrestled for a bit and he gave me a gigantic fight and people came out on their porches. And some were crying and others were yelling to call animal control and even more were saying, "Is that Olivia?"

Yes, it was me. It was me. Just me.

And even as the jaws of the deadly animal were about to bite my butt off, even then, I maintained my composure, kept the thing at arm's length and managed to contain it in a soon-to-be-recycled Tang jug.

Everyone cheered.

Bonnie was dead.

And Carlene came and hugged me.

Bonnie stared.

"What's wrong with you," she said.

I said.

I said . . . I tried to say something.

"Do you have a mental disorder?"

I felt like I couldn't breathe.

Then she said, "Lala said your dad is a LOSER and that he just took off and that he made a bunch of people mad."

A LOSER.

I looked at Carlene who was looking at her hands. I had never heard her or Lala say anything like that.

I thought I was going to throw up and I probably was going to.

When Dad left, everyone was nice to us, and Tandi got us a gift card for Dominos and came over, and Mom cried and I said, "He said he'd be back. He's just gone for a bit."

But Mom kept crying and Tandi said, "Go on to your room, honey."

A LOSER.

I looked back at Bonnie who had bad breath and I said, "He's coming back. He's in Bryce Canyon is all. He's coming back."

Bonnie blew a bubble and popped it. Then she said, "Is that where his girlfriend lives?"

"His girlfriend?" I looked at Carlene.

She wouldn't look at me.

"What are you talking about?"

Now Bonnie was looking at Carlene, too. "She doesn't know?"

Carlene said, "Lala was just being stupid. She makes stuff up."

My heart was pounding. What did Lala say? What was going on?

"That's not what you said yesterday," Bonnie said.

We both waited as Carlene did nothing but pick at her fingers and then cough. And cough and cough.

Finally, I said, "He doesn't have a stupid girlfriend. He just went away for a job and he's coming home."

Bonnie nudged Carlene. "Tell her what Lala was saying."

I looked at Carlene. "What was Lala saying?"

Carlene was bright red now. "I don't want to talk about this."

But Bonnie kept going, she said, "Lala said your dad was trashy. She said your dad was trashy trashy trashy."

Carlene looked at me and I was trying not to cry. I was trying not to do anything.

"And gross," she said.

Bonnie looked almost happy that she was saying all this. That she thought she knew something that I didn't and I didn't even know Bonnie so why did she care? And my dad didn't have a girlfriend.

He was my dad.

He was married.

To my mom.

And he went to Bryce Canyon.

He was in Bryce Canyon.

By himself.

Bonnie started to say something. I don't even know what because before she could get out a word, Carlene said, "Shut up, Bonnie."

Just like that.

Shut up, you dumb-bum Bonnie.

Bonnie looked stunned and I was kind of surprised, too, because Carlene didn't usually say things like shut up.

Carlene had sweat beads on her forehead and she was breathing through her nose.

Bonnie's face turned hard, like you could see her eyes get black and she said, "You shut up."

She stood up.

So then Carlene stood up.

"This place sucks," Bonnie said.

And Carlene said, "Sorry. I didn't mean it."

And Bonnie said, "I knew I shouldn't have come here. It gives me the creeps."

And Carlene said, "I'm so sorry."

And she said, "I'm calling my mom."

And Carlene said, "We have Ding Dongs. Do you want a Ding Dong?"

Bonnie ignored her. She stalked into Carlene's house with Carlene begging her not to leave.

I sat there.

A girlfriend?

Did he have a girlfriend?

Was he trashy?

And gross? What did that even mean?

I took a breath.

He was not trashy and this is what was happening to me in the middle of Saturday and Berkeley and Mom were on errands and I was alone and Dad was in Bryce Canyon.

~

Please, Dad. Be in Bryce Canyon. Riding around on horses. Going on hikes. Helping people.

Please don't be gone because you're trashy and gross.

And a loser.

CHAPTER 16

When Mom and Berk got home that night, Mom was tired.

Berkeley wanted me to read to her and Mom said, "I'm going to bed."

"I need to talk to you."

I'd been waiting all day.

Waiting and waiting and waiting.

She looked at me. "Is something wrong?"

Something was wrong. Something was very wrong.

I'd been planning it. What I'd say.

Is Dad gone for good?

Does he love someone else?

Is he trashy and gross?

Is he a loser?

She had purple rings under her eyes.

She and Berkeley had gotten thirty-six dollars at the recycling center from cans me and Berk had collected from around the trailer court and over at the KOA. They'd gone to five different stores because of coupons and Mom had a fight with the car repairman. "Mom yelled at him," Berk said.

And Mom said, "I did not yell at him."

And Berkeley said, "He told you to stop yelling at him."

And Mom sighed. "I guess I got mad."

So she yelled at a car repairman.

"What's wrong," she asked me.

She looked like bones. Just bones.

And I said . . .

I said nothing.

Then she went to bed and Berkeley said, "Will you read me *Corduroy*?"

I looked over at my Berk. Curled up in Dad's big chair.

"Okay," I said.

"Okay," she said.

And I read about Corduroy and his lost button.

CHAPTER 17

In the middle of the night I wrote a note for Carlene. It said this:

> *Why did Lala say that? Do you think my dad is a loser?*

I also put: *I still want to go to Monster Jam.*

I stared at it.

Then I ripped it up.

Maybe my dad was trash and if she didn't want to talk about it, neither did I.

I crossed off Monster Jam on my calendar.

CHAPTER 18

The next day went by and I couldn't get it out of my mind.

Trashy.

Loser.

Gross.

Girlfriend.

Ugh.

Berk and I did our usual routine and no Bart and no nothing.

I didn't feel like eating the maple bars Delilah brought us and when Mrs. Sydney Gunnerson stopped by the tramp to say she'd teach me how to sing some songs because I'd asked her about that a while back because I thought maybe I'd go on *The Voice* and at first she'd said she had no time but now she said she would do it but I just said, "No thanks."

She put her hand on her hip and got a look on her face. She was wearing a turban on her head.

"I will not offer again, young lady."

And I looked at her face. She had thick black glasses and wiry hairs coming out of her chin, but she was kind of pretty in an old lady kind of way.

I wondered if she was trashy and gross.

"No thank you," I said again.

Berkeley said, "I will."

And Mrs. Sydney Gunnerson said Berkeley's voice wasn't mature enough yet.

And then she left.

I sort of regretted saying no to her because then I'd get to see the inside of her trailer firsthand and because of *The Voice* but I also didn't regret it because I felt like throwing up.

We sat on the tramp.

We read our books.

We ate our stupid sandwiches.

I watched Grant and Bob walk around. Grant was trying to fix something on his car and swore.

And Berkeley yelled, "That's a bad word" and I wished she would just be quiet but Grant looked over and said, "Did you say something?" and Berkeley said, "That was a bad word," and Grant laughed and said, "Sorry, I'll try to watch my language," and Berkeley said, "You really should," and then he laughed again and then burped, which I thought was kind of rude.

I also knew for sure Bart was a liar. The FBI would have no interest in someone like Grant.

So that's how the week went.

Boring and nothing.

Except Paul did show me two MMA moves called the Double Leg Takedown, which I tried out, and Paul said, "Dang girl," because I was actually pretty good at it, and also the Spinning Back Fist, which I need to practice.

And I got a job taking out Wanda and Jerry Smith's garbage each week for a dollar because Jerry, who usually does it, twisted his ankle at Petco when he was trying to clean out the cat cages and Wanda doesn't leave her house.

But other than those things, boring. And nothing.

The weekend was even worse.

On Saturday, Carlene and Bonnie were giggling on Carlene's front porch and I came out and said hi.

And then they both stopped laughing and Bonnie said, "We have to go," and she took Carlene's hand and they went inside.

I could see them go to Carlene's room through the windows and they turned on music and they were probably going to the mall soon.

I wondered if Bonnie was invited to the Monster Jam.

Mom and Berk were inside.

We were supposed to go swimming at the rec center later but I didn't feel like it.

Delilah came by in her jogging outfit even though she doesn't jog and she said, "What's troubling you, hon?"

I said, "Nothing."

And she said, "Don't look like nothing."

So I ignored her and went and sat on the tramp.

Then I got off the tramp.

Then I walked to the KOA to see if anything was going on there.

Nothing.

Except a couple sitting on a picnic table feeding each other doughnuts, which made me feel like barfing all over them.

Dad didn't have a girlfriend.

No way he had a girlfriend.

I walked back.

Nobody interesting was on the trail and it was Little League practice at the fields; not that I cared ever who was over there except for one time there was a family reunion and they brought a band that played Taylor Swift and I liked it.

Blah.

Nothing.

So I sat on the tramp and knew in my whole life nothing was ever going to happen and I was going to rot and die.

I thought that, but I also thought how deep down in a place between my intestines and stomach, in a small little pocket, a voice was telling me that someday I'd see Bart again.

That he'd come.

That he'd understand.

That he was different like me.

That we both had big ideas and were going to big places.

Not to give up.

And I said, "I don't even care about him. Give up what?"

And the voice said, "You know."

And I said, "I do not know."

And the voice said, "You know."

And I said, "No, I don't."

And I was getting very angry at this voice because I didn't even care about Bart anymore. Just then a marching band came down our street.

CHAPTER 19

This was the biggest marching band I had ever seen. Bigger than the one on the Fourth of July. Bigger than the one on TV at Thanksgiving.

Bigger than if the universe had a marching band and it was populated with people and animals and small trucks.

They were playing a song.

And someone was singing, someone with a horrible loud voice.

People on their way to work said, Baby what did you expect. Gonna burst into flame, go ahead.

And just then, in the middle of the trombones and the saxophones and the tubas, just then, around the corner came an elephant, and on top of the elephant was Bart. Standing with a microphone and pointing at me. "There she is, ladies and gentlemen," he said.

I laughed.

He smiled.

The band stopped marching but they didn't stop playing.

Bart said, "Your dad doesn't have a girlfriend but I do."

I laughed.

He motioned for me to come on top of the elephant with him.

"How?" I yelled, and he pointed at a rope ladder.

So then I did. I climbed the rope ladder and jumped into his arms and he threw down the microphone and right there, in the middle of our street with the music playing and Carlene and dumb-bum Bonnie and Chip and Tandi and Jerry and Wanda Smith and Baby George and Delilah and Paul and Mrs. Sydney Gunnerson and Fancy Melody and Harry and Bob and Grant and everyone, especially Mom, watching, me and Bart kissed and kissed and kissed.

I sat on the burning tramp and knew that maybe the voice was right.

I would see him again.

I had an idea.

CHAPTER 20

I asked Mom if I could go to the library.

"Again? Now?"

"Yes," I said.

"We're going to the pool."

"Can you drop me off?"

She looked at me. Then at Berk. "You want to be dropped off at the library?"

She was acting like it was the weirdest thing she'd ever heard.

"Yes, please," I said. "While you guys swim. I need to get some studying done."

She stared at me.

I said, "I'm trying to stay at grade level."

Even though she didn't let me go to school, things like that always got to her.

"Grade level?" she said.

"Yeah," I said. "So I can be in seventh grade next year."

She bit her lip.

"Maybe it's for the best," she said.

I said, "It's really for the best."

So she dropped me off.

~

When I got there I did four things.

1. I got a drink. They have the coldest best water there.
2. I picked out a DVD called *The Buttercream Gang* for me and Berk for later.
3. I waited in line for a computer and then I entered a sweepstakes called *Lights, Camera, Switzerland!* and one called *TJ Maxx Dazzle in Diamonds* and then *Big and Rich's Las Vegas Run Away With You Weekend*— in case I didn't get to go to Monster Jam after all.
4. And then for the most important reason to be there, I Googled Steve Fossett. Which felt like it might bring Bart back.

Bart was right.

Steve Fossett was the best person ever.

He went around the world in a hot-air balloon.

He hiked almost all the highest peaks in the world except Everest, which I wouldn't want to hike that one because you could lose your fingers at the least or turn into a Popsicle and die at the most.

He swam to Alcatraz.

And he raced cars.

He flew a fixed-wing airplane around the world nonstop.

The only bad thing about him was he went out on a solo flight one day and then disappeared.

Thousands of people searched for him. Thousands and thousands.

For months.

For years.

But he was gone. Without a trace.

And then, after looking and looking and looking, his wife had him declared legally dead.

It was very mysterious.

I wish it had stayed like that. Legally dead but no evidence.

Maybe he escaped to the woods and was living as a mountain man. Maybe he'd trekked to Antarctica and had built an igloo castle. Maybe he hitchhiked to New York City and was a musician on the streets.

He could be anywhere. Doing anything.

But then one day, a hiker ruined it.

He found a bone.

Steve Fossett's bone according to DNA.

I sat at the computer and stared at his picture and then the picture of the bone. He had disappeared without a trace but then they found a bone.

A teeny tiny bone. All that was left.

I didn't know whether to laugh or to cry.

CHAPTER 21

That night, after they went to the rec center and I found out about Steve Fossett, Mom said, "I'm going out."

I was eating ramen.

Berk was in the street playing with the Johnson girls.

Carlene was nowhere.

"Out?"

Mom was wearing tight jeans and a shimmery shirt.

"What's that?" I said.

"What?"

"That," I said, pointing to her shirt.

She looked down. "It's my blouse."

"I've never seen it."

She shrugged. "Do you like it?"

I stared at her. Her hair was loose and she had on thick red lipstick.

She looked how I was going to look when I had my first kiss and it made me kind of mad.

"Who you going out with?" I said, ignoring the question.

"Tandi. And Chelsea."

She fixed her hair in the reflection on the microwave.

"I thought you hated Tandi."

She sighed. "I don't hate Tandi. We just had a disagreement."

It was more than a disagreement though. Everything was normal and then one day they had a fight and Mom wasn't speaking to her. Tandi even came over and Mom wouldn't let us open the door.

But now they were going out together.

"Chip is letting Tandi go out?"

Mom looked at me. "Why wouldn't Chip let Tandi go out?"

I shrugged.

She turned now and faced me.

"Why would you say that? Tandi can do whatever she wants."

Her face was red and I didn't know why and I said, "I just meant, I thought Tandi and Chip have date night on Saturdays."

Mom looked like she didn't know this.

"They do?"

"Carlene said they do. And that they make out."

"They make out?"

I nodded. "Carlene said they go on a date and then they come home and make out."

Mom smiled. Then she turned back to the microwave.

"I don't know what they usually do but she's going out with me tonight."

I sat there.

Then Mom said, "Put Berkeley to bed by nine, okay?"

"Where are you going?" I asked.

She looked at me. "I already told you. Out."

"Out where?"

"Out."

I tried to imagine my mom out. Out at a bowling alley for laser glow-in-the-dark bowling and she gets a strike and everyone cheers and a man named Carl picks her up and puts her on his shoulders.

Out at *Los Hermanos* to eat chips and salsa and then someone says, "Sing! Sing! Sing!" because my mom used to be in a band and she used to play the banjo and she'd have gigs that we went to and I thought she was the prettiest woman in the world. Now I didn't think that as much.

Or more probably, she'd go to *Lamars,* the pool lounge where I knew Dad went and sometimes Mom.

I hoped they wouldn't go to *Lamars.*

What I really wanted was for her to stay home.

To watch the *Buttercream Gang* with us.

To make caramel popcorn and let me put my head in her lap and then she'd braid my hair.

I wanted her to tell us stories about her grandma's

house, which was way in the country and had horses and stables and a pond where you could swim.

And I could be sad that I never got to go there because she died before I was born and Mom would be sad, too, and we'd be sad together.

I wanted her to not go out with dumb Tandi and whoever else was maybe saying my dad was trash.

She grabbed her keys.

"Go to sleep by eleven," she said, and then she walked out the door.

I went to sleep at twelve thirty on the couch.

I have no idea when she got home.

CHAPTER 22

One problem is when there's no floor.

Like you're walking around and you don't even care about where you're going to step because you've never had to worry about it before.

And then out of the blue, on a Monday, or a Tuesday, or maybe a Wednesday, the most boring days of the week, when the sky is gray and everything is happening how it always happens, on one of those days, suddenly you take a step and the ground is gone.

And you're falling

And falling

And falling.

A bad part is there's no warning.

No one tells you.

And even worse, it *seems* like the ground is there.

That it will always be there.

It looks like regular old carpet or grass or cement or tile or dirt or rock. Right there, under your feet.

But then you take a step, and you fall right through.

Saturday night was bad.

Monday morning was no ground.

CHAPTER 23

Berkeley and I were at breakfast.

I thought I'd go to the library again. I wanted to write down all the records Steve Fossett had.

Maybe I'd try one. Maybe I'd fly around the world in a balloon. Or climb a mountain.

I also wanted to look up student exchange programs and enter some more contests. I was way behind.

I thought Berk and I could eat lunch and wait at the park by the library until three thirty when the elementary got out. Then we were safe to go in the library and we could stay there until dinner.

I was planning this all out when Mom said, "Hurry and finish, you're going to be late for school."

Berkeley and I both stopped eating. "What?"

She was looking at her phone.

"Mom?"

"What?"

"School?"

She nodded, still not looking at me. "School."

Then she said to Berkeley, "You need to get ready, too."

"Where am I going?" Berk said.

"Day care," Mom said, like it was normal. Like of course she was going to day care and of course I was going to school even though I hadn't been in weeks and maybe months and was probably already kicked out.

"I can watch her, Mom," I said. Like this was some new idea.

"She doesn't have a cough anymore," she said back. We were in a fake conversation about a fake world and everything that was happening was fake.

Mom walked out of the kitchen to the bathroom.

I felt sick. Berkeley looked pale herself.

"Hang on," I whispered to her. "I'll go fix this."

Mom was in the bathroom.

I walked in and sat on the closed toilet.

"It's okay, I can watch her," I said again.

Mom was studying her face in the mirror.

"Okay, Mom?"

"The school called," she said. "You have to go."

The school called. The school called. The school called.

They'd called before when I first stopped going and Mom said, "Just don't answer it." We had a home line back then because Mom didn't pay her cell.

But now she had a cell and I guess they found out her number.

"Tell them I'm homeschooled," I said.

"You're not homeschooled," she said.

She was picking at something below her nose.

"You can say I'm homeschooled. Lots of people are homeschooled."

"You're not homeschooled," she said again. "We're a regular family. I go to work. You go to school. Your sister goes to day care."

I felt something hot start to burn in my stomach.

We were not a regular family.

Not.

A regular.

Family.

At all.

She got out her lipstick. Pink this time. Why was she doing this to me?

"School is out in, like, two months," I said. "I won't have time to catch up. I don't think I should go back," I said.

She leaned into the mirror.

"Mom."

"I don't want to go back."

She leaned closer.

"Mom."

"Mom."

"Mom."

"Mom?"

"Mom!"

"What?!" She slammed down the eyeliner. I took a step back, her voice so loud. "What? Why are you shouting? I can't stand shouting." She was breathing hard. "Go sit in time-out."

I stood there. My heart thumping.

"Go," she said.

"What?"

"GO SIT IN TIME-OUT."

She was serious.

She was putting me in time-out.

"GO!"

I tried to be okay. I tried to just be normal. I tried to turn around and sit in time-out, which I guess was the corner where she put Berkeley sometimes.

I tried to do that but I felt like I couldn't breathe and I couldn't look at her and I tried to do what she said and I thought, I can't do this.

Then I went and sat in the corner in time-out.

I wish Bart would have at least left me his phone number or email.

I wish I could tell him please come to my house.

Please.

I will run a hundred miles.

I will cut my hair into a Mohawk.

I will eat hard candy all day.

I will do anything.

I will go anywhere.

Please.

She dropped me off at school.

In the front.

Like it was normal.

She gave me two bucks for lunch.

Told me to walk home.

"Walk home?"

"It's only a few miles," she said.

She was not looking at me.

She used to pick me up from school. Everyone got picked up from school.

"A few miles," I whispered. "Okay."

And then as I was getting out, she grabbed my arm and said, "Olivia?"

I tried not to cry.

"I'm sorry."

Right then I thought maybe she'd change her mind. Maybe I could get back in the car and we could all go to McDonald's and then she could go to work and me and Berkeley could go home and everything would be normal.

But then she said, "You know where the key is."

My lip trembled.

She gave me a hard look. "Don't get any ideas. Don't skip. You have to do this or they're going to make me go to court."

I stared at her. "Court?"

She nodded. "Court. And maybe jail."

My heart thumped. They wouldn't put her in jail would they? Not really.

"Do this for me, baby girl. Okay?"

I nodded.

And then she waved me away and she and Berkeley took off down the road, leaving me in front of Dixon Middle School.

Just then a spaceship landed.

I got in.

I flew away.

I never came back.

I have been to four states including Utah.

Colorado, Arizona, and Idaho.

My goal is to go to every state in the country.

That was another reason why I really wanted to go to Las Vegas with Carlene.

One time I heard on TV that you could be an exchange student in the United States. Like if you wanted to go to school in Texas or Minnesota or even Hawaii and you were from stupid Utah, all you had to do was apply and then go live with a family and be their kid for the year and go to a whole new school and eat lobsters if you were in Maine.

I thought Maine might be good.

I told Berkeley that and she said, "They have lobsters in Maine?"

And then she asked me, "Why would you want lobsters?"

I had to explain and then she said she thought that was a good idea but she wouldn't want to eat lobsters.

And I said, "I think you'd like them," even though I'd never eaten one or even a shrimp in my life.

Next time I got to the library I was going to apply.

....

Dear Dad,

I went back to school today. It was really fun to see all my friends. I've been staying home a little bit because of Berkeley's cough but now I'm back.

We only have two more months left so I have a lot of things to finish. One is a report on an animal native to Utah. I wondered if you had a good idea for that? I was thinking an animal you encounter a lot at Bryce? Wolves? Skunks? Bears?

Also, I might be coming to summer school to help some of the other students. I'm excited! I wanted to know what dates we might come visit you or if you're coming here, when that is so that I can make sure summer school isn't at the same time.

Do you think you'll go to Monster Jam in Las Vegas? I haven't talked to Carlene about it in a while. Do you ever talk to Chip? Maybe you could see if it's still okay if I go?

Also, that boy Bart may have been abducted.

I hope you get back to your ranger station or whatever it is soon to get this letter. Am I sending them to the right place?

Love, Olivia

....

CHAPTER 28

When I got home from school that day, no one was home.

I'd walked by myself on the river trail even though I thought maybe I could walk with Carlene but I couldn't find her.

I did see dumb-bum Bonnie out waiting for her ride but who cares about that.

I walked and I watched the river moving fast and suddenly I fell in it.

I was screaming and I was going to die, the water choking me and every time I tried to swim, an undercurrent would pull me farther.

There were people on the bank. Hugging and crying.

"Help me," I cried.

But no one dared because the water was ice cold and the current swift.

More people showed up.

And I thought this is how I'm going to die.

Then I thought: I almost died in the pool before.

And then I thought: I am going to die in water.

And then I thought: What if I died in the bathtub?

And then there were voices.

"Somebody save her!"

"Somebody jump in!"

But nobody jumped in.

And I said, "Dear God. Thanks for the good times. At least it's not the tub."

But then, right before I went under, right before a huge news helicopter spun overhead, right then, I got a surge of energy.

I swam across the rushing water, my body almost like a fish. People cheering. Bart yelling.

Bart?

Bart was there.

He was there and he held a big towel that said, GO OLIVIA!!

And Berkeley was jumping up and down. Dad was giving Mom a piggyback, which was weird but kind of romantic.

And Carlene and Lala and dumb-bum Bonnie and Chip and Tandi and even Delilah were sitting on Chip's monster truck cheering.

And this time, when I got out, nobody had to give me CPR. But Bart kissed me. Again.

In front of everyone.

Again.

Even Troy the lifeguard was there and he looked on in jealousy.

Then I tripped on a rock and fell down and scraped my knee.

My first day back where no one talked to me and where I knew I was never going to pass sixth grade and where I tried to pretend like I didn't care.

When I got home, there was a huge sign out in the quad that said HOME OWNERS ASSOCIATION MEETING TONIGHT and there was a picture of a duck on it, which is a long story.

For some reason, this cheered me up almost as much as drowning in the river.

One time right after Dad left, the Home Owners Association, which is now run by Mrs. Sydney Gunnerson, sent out a satisfaction survey.

Mom said who cares and threw it in the garbage. This made me feel bad because Mom used to be the HOA president and in charge of the whole thing.

She used to make sure there was a potluck on Labor Day.

She organized fish fries when Dad got back from his trips with his buddies.

She even had a luau one year.

But now she wasn't president and when the survey came asking what activities we wanted to do and how we hoped the year would go, she threw it way.

Who cares.

Who cares.

Who cares.

Berkeley and I sat there as Mom put on her jacket, looked at herself in the mirror, and went out. Again.

I got the survey out of the garbage. Found a pen.

"What are you doing?" Berk asked.

I said, "What are *you* doing?"

And she said, "Watching you."

And I said, "I'm making our life better."

And she said, "That's good," and went back to her dolls.

I opened the pen and answered the questions. Yes, we wanted more activities. Yes, we wanted better flowers. Yes, we were willing to contribute to the birthday pot. And no, we did not feel that time and money was better spent on putting in a new septic tank whatever that was.

At the end I wrote: *I would like to have some parties. I am very busy at my work so I can't organize them anymore. However, my daughters can help. Please include them in any planning. I will make sure they don't disappoint the board.*

Sincerely,

LeAnn Hales

Berkeley said, "What did you write?"

And I said, "That we should have parties."

She said, "Yes. And Popsicles."

So I put, *"And Popsicles."*

CHAPTER 31

I went to the HOA meeting that night. The night of my first time back to school.

I hoped they were going to talk about possible festivals and decorating ideas and whether it was a good idea to get a pool.

Instead they talked about taxes and how no one is doing their garbage time right and also about sewage.

It was boring.

Everything in life was boring.

CHAPTER 32

That night, Berk whispered up to me from the bunk below, "Did you have a good day."

The stars were out bright and I'd been watching for planes.

I didn't think she was awake.

Did I have a good day? I'd been trying not to think about it.

My eyes started to water. "It was okay," I said.

She was quiet.

Then she said, "I hate day care."

I nodded to myself. I'd hate it, too.

"They don't have art like we do," she said. "Just stupid coloring books."

I nodded again, a tear slipping down my cheek.

"And the lady told me that no one puts chips in their tuna sandwiches so I wasn't allowed."

"Just a plain sandwich then?"

"I put some in anyway," she said. "It felt more like home."

I laughed.

Then she said, "How long do I have to go?"

"I don't know," I said.

She was quiet then.

For a long time.

People were laughing outside. Someone yelled. A truck drove by. The usual.

She said, "Did the HOA say they were doing any parties for the neighborhood?"

I sighed. Ugh. Blah. No.

But instead I said, "Yes. They want us to plan a summer bash."

"Really?" she said. "Us?"

I closed my eyes. Tight. "Really."

"What kind of bash?"

What kind what kind what kind what kind?

"Uh, they want like a circus."

She gasped. "A circus?"

I smiled. "Not a real circus, you know, but like entertainment and popcorn and lemonade."

"And cotton candy," she said. "Sadie and Jane have been to Ringling Brothers and she said they got cotton candy."

"For sure," I said. "Maybe we could rent one of those machines," and even as I said it, I knew I should stop. Say, "Just kidding." Say, "Ha-ha." Say, say, anything but tell her no. There would be no circus.

None.

Nope.

But then I didn't and Berkeley she kept going. "I bet I could tightrope." There were people over at the softball park lately who put up a kind of rope between two trees and practiced walking and doing tricks on it. Berkeley and I had watched them for hours one day.

"You could."

"And you can juggle."

"Not really," I said. I'd tried a few times with oranges.

She got quiet then and I got quiet then.

The night filled our room and I suddenly felt alone. And cold. And no one.

Like who cares?

Who cares?

No one cares.

Just me and Berk.

Alone.

Then out of the darkness she whispered, "I love you, Livy."

I really started crying then. We never said things like that and I don't know why but we never did.

"Liv?" she said, because I was taking too long to try not to sob. "Are you still awake?"

I took a long breath, wiped my nose and my eyes. Then I said to my sweet little sister, "I love you, too," I said.

Then she said, "What if we pray."

"What if we what?" I said.

"What if we pray that it will work out?"

What will work out? I wondered. What did she want to work out? No more school for me? No more day care for her? Mom and Dad? Our family? What did she want?

What did I want?

Then she said, "What if we pray that we really can have a circus."

I laughed. "I think that's a good idea."

And she said, "I'll start now."

....

Dear Dad,

There is a man named Steve Fossett. He disappeared. And then they found out he was dead.

I still want to go get waffles with you. Berk and I and Mom miss you. Please come back.

We might be doing a circus. Maybe you could come help us.

Love,
Olivia

P.S. If you are not getting these letters, I wish I knew.

....

CHAPTER 33

Each day, Mom and Berkeley dropping me off, Berk giving me a secret look, and me winking back. I knew she was praying because I could hear her each night.

Please let us have a real circus.

Please let there be cotton candy.

Please let there be a tiger.

I also knew she was practicing her tightrope on a jump rope on our floor and that she'd already told Sadie and Jane who said they could help.

"They know a lot about circuses," she told me.

"I'm sure they do," I said.

Then she'd make me practice juggling, which I was getting pretty good at.

Those were the best parts of the day.

The worst part of the day were the mornings.

Mom and Berk would drop me off and I had to face a whole day stretched out in front of me.

Alone.

Class.

Class.

Fifteen-minute break-sit in the library.

Class.

Lunch.

Class.

Class.

Class.

Every. Single. Day.

I didn't talk to people much because I didn't feel like it.

In some ways, I just blended in. No worries.

But then I won a major award.

CHAPTER 34

It happened when I was at lunch and I was sitting by myself and then all these girls like Carlene and Bonnie and Chrissie Tolman, who is the new student body president for next year I just found out, and who learned my name my first day back, which made me excited, and then a boy said, "She knows everyone's name. That's what she does," and I said, "Oh."

Anyway, all of the girls I know and lots of girls I didn't know came to my table.

"You've won a major award," Chrissie said.

One girl, a redhead named Sasha, she started to cry.

"What's wrong?" I asked the others.

"She was up for the award but you got the most votes."

I was going to ask what it was for but then the principal was on the loudspeaker and said she had a special announcement. "One of our very own students has been picked to live in Portland, Maine!"

Everyone gasped.

"This only happens to one out of every 345,908 sixth graders."

Chrissie and Carlene and Bonnie and all the girls around me started patting me on the back and I was nodding and thanking them and I felt bad for Sasha and I said, "I'm so sorry." And she said, "You deserve it."

And then the principal said, "Instead of announcing it myself, I have invited someone very special to do the honors for me."

The whole lunchroom was silent and I wondered if it'd be Beyoncé or maybe the president of the United States.

And then, after a few seconds, a man's voice came on.

My dad's voice.

My dad.

And he said, "Don't go, Olivia! Come to Bryce Canyon with me! I miss you so much! Don't go to Maine and eat lobsters."

I wanted to go to Maine to eat lobsters.

Of course I did.

But I knew, even though the girls were all staring at me, some holding hands, others whispering, Maine, Maine, Maine, Maine, even through all that, I knew, with all my heart, that I was meant to ride around on a horse with my dad at Bryce Canyon.

And that's when someone threw a hamburger patty at my head.

CHAPTER 35

Hamburgers are delicious.

One time our whole family, including the dog because Dad brought one home once but then it got smashed by a semi on the highway, one time, my whole family went to Granny's restaurant for hamburgers up the canyon.

It was my best day.

The windows down.

The music loud.

And a fancy meal.

Cheeseburger, tomatoes, lettuce, onions, thick fries with cups and cups of fry sauce, and a Butterfinger shake to go with it.

Berkeley said, "Can we do this again?" as she took a huge bite of her gummy-bear shake.

And Mom laughed and Dad smiled and said, "Of course we can. Of course we will."

Of course.

Of course.

Of course.

~

Now there was ketchup on my face but not onions or tomatoes or lettuce because we don't have those kind of hamburgers at school and fifty thousand people staring at me, and I sat there.

And someone said, "Who threw it?"

And someone else said, "Who is that?" because no one knows who I am.

And someone else was laughing.

Most people were actually.

And I was trying to sit there.

And not cry.

Just sit there.

And maybe start eating my chef salad that I bought for 1.56 plus tax.

Should I keep eating?

Should I stand up?

Should I go to the bathroom?

Should someone come over here and tell me what to do?

Or should they sit there and laugh and talk about it and then go back to their food and their friends and yelling so and so and something and something.

What should I do?

Then there was someone.

A lunch lady named Edna who said, "Come on,

sweetie." And she took me to the back of the cafeteria where she and all the workers were.

I left my chef salad on the table without one bite. 1.56 plus tax gone. I wanted to shove it in my backpack but I didn't have time.

She said, "Are you okay?"

I said, "Yes."

They were done serving so they were cleaning up and Edna said, "Lisa, throw me a clean cloth."

Lisa was a lady with braces and she smiled and I smiled back and then she threw the cloth.

While I was wiping my face, Edna was talking to me.

She was saying things like, "Those darn kids." And, "They don't have a cell in their brains and when I was your age I got the treatment, too. It was relentless and all because I had headgear. Do you know what headgear is?" and no, I did not know what headgear was but Lisa the other lunch lady did. And then Edna was saying that it was going to get better when I was older. That there'd be a time where I would see those same little-brained kids on the street and point my finger and say look how you turned out and look how I turned out and then I could laugh.

She was telling me all these things while I was wiping my face.

And she was still talking when I looked over to the

dishwasher area because a kid yelled something and that's when I saw Bart.

With a hairnet on his head.

And he saw me.

CHAPTER 36

After the hamburger patty and after I said, "HEY," and Edna said, "Who you shouting at," and Bart took off and went out a door and I said, "Who was that?" And she said, "Who was who?" And I said, "Bart?" And she said, "I don't know a Bart," and I said, "That kid washing dishes?" and she said, "Harrison?" And I said, "His name is Bart I thought," And she said, "That was one of our student helpers, Harrison." And then she said, "I don't know a Bart except there was a Bartholomew in my community ceramics class two years ago and he was a character. He had a full beard and a wonderful sense of humor and we may or may not have spent a little time getting to know each other, if you know what I mean," and then she and Lisa were laughing and I had most of the ketchup off my head, after that, I left.

CHAPTER 37

I said, "Life is stupid."

And Melody said, "Don't say that."

I was drinking ginger ale and eating cookies and saying life was stupid and she was telling me not to say life was stupid even though she sat on the steps of her trailer and cried all day and all night and her husband, Harry, was nowhere, just like my dad was nowhere. I'd seen her sitting there after school and for no reason I decided to talk to her and for no reason she got me ginger ale and cookies.

I said, "It is."

She said, "It's not."

I said, "It's not?"

She said, "It's not."

I said, "Today someone threw a hamburger at my head."

She paused. "A real hamburger?"

I thought about what a fake hamburger would be like. Maybe one of those candy ones?

But it was real so I said, "Yep."

"Really?"

Then I told her the whole thing. I told her how I sat there.

I told her how I had to go in the kitchen part of the cafeteria while everyone watched or didn't watch.

I told her about Lisa and Edna with the headgear.

I did not tell her about Bart or Harrison or whoever he was.

She sighed.

Then I kept talking.

It was like I couldn't stop.

I told her about how I had to go back to school and I hadn't been going to school but now I had to and it was the worst.

I told her how I was behind and how I had no friends but that I didn't even try to get friends because it felt tiring and maybe I'd get to stay home again soon. I even told her how I made up a circus for Berkeley and how that was never going to happen. I told her that every day of my life—Every. Single. Day.—of my life was stupid.

It was the first time I opened my mouth and let anything that wanted to just come spilling out.

When I was done.

And I was breathing hard.

And probably sunburned.

When I was done, she was quiet.

Didn't say a thing.

I waited.

I wondered what kind of perfume she was wearing.

A fly landed on my leg. I slapped at it. It flew away.

Then Melody said, "What if that had been a butterfly?"

I looked at her. "What?"

"Would you have swatted it if it'd been a butterfly?"

"Uh," I thought about it. Would I have? "Probably not," I said.

She nodded. Then she said, "Why not?"

"Because butterflies are good. Flies are bad."

She said, "Are they?"

I took a bite of cookie. Then she said, "Flies can be gross. They can spread disease and infest meat and grain."

"That's what I mean," I said.

"But . . ." She cut me off. "They also pollinate more plants, including food that you would never guess. They do just as much good as the bees do and not only that, they feed hummingbirds, sparrows, and songbirds."

I had no idea why she was talking about this. Who cared about the dumb flies? Also I didn't know they did that kind of thing. But still.

She took a cookie off the plate. "People decide things without knowing the whole story. Usually things aren't all one way or all the other way. Usually they're a little bit of everything."

I thought about that for a few seconds while she ate another cookie.

Then she said, "A hamburger?"

I said, "What?"

And she said, "They threw a hamburger?"

And I said, "A hamburger."

She said, "Cheeseburger?"

I said, "Hamburger. They don't have cheeseburgers at my school." I also said, "They may not have been aiming at me."

And she said, "That's the spirit."

Then I said, "Is Harry coming back?"

She sat back and closed her eyes. "Maybe. Maybe not."

Then she said, "You weren't going to school?"

I said, "No."

She said, "Your mom knew you weren't going to school? Do you guys get money from the government? They can help with day care."

My stomach started to bubble a little because Mom won't do anything like that and says we don't need other people's money and it's none of anyone's business and we can take care of ourselves and here I was telling Melody, which Mom would hate hate hate so I said, "Where does Harry go?"

She sighed. "I don't know."

I took a drink of ginger ale. I thought about me. I thought about Mom. I also thought about Harry and Melody.

I wanted to ask if Harry was bad. Or good. Or if he was a little bit of everything.

I wanted to ask if he was the reason she sat out here for hours. Or if she loved him even though he left all the time or if *he* loved *her* even when he left all the time or if they talked or if he had a girlfriend that wasn't her or if she thought about moving to Virginia or if she killed flies in her kitchen or let them lay eggs all over the place and multiply so that they could pollinate food and plants I would never guess and get eaten by songbirds. Maybe her house was filled with songbirds.

Maybe she and Harry loved each other so much.

Maybe she and Harry hated each other so much.

I wanted to ask her everything.

But then I decided not to ask her anything.

Instead we sat in the sun.

Then she said, "I know how to ride a unicycle."

....

Dear Dad,

I talked to Melody today. Do you remember her? It turns out she does stunt work and hair and makeup for local movies which there aren't a lot of but she used to live in LA and she did it all the time there. A stunt person! Plus, hair and makeup. One time she was a double on a superhero movie but she couldn't tell me which one for privacy reasons. I think it was Thor. Or Batman. But I don't know.

I told her how great school is going. She also said she could do my hair for free because she's in between jobs right now and she needs to practice so we might dye it because Mom doesn't do that anymore. She also said she could permanently straighten it. Like a reverse perm. Should I do that? Mom said I shouldn't but Mom and Melody are different.

I hope you are good and that you like being a ranger at Bryce Canyon where I know you are. That boy Bart is definitely a liar.

Sincerely,

Your daughter,
Olivia

P.S. He's not dead or abducted.

....

CHAPTER 38

The next day after the hamburger was a Saturday, which I was glad for.

Even though I had gone to school for two weeks and I was starting to be okay for the most part, I was relieved to get a day off.

A day to sit on my tramp.

Mom didn't have to work in the morning again so she got up early and by the time me and Berkeley were awake she was already scrubbing the kitchen, which she used to do back before but which she hadn't done for a long long time.

She didn't like to bring work home with her.

The whole place smelled like lemon.

She said, "Get dressed, girls. We're going out for breakfast."

Berkeley said, "What?"

And she said, "You heard me. As soon as I get this floor done, I'm getting in the car and getting me a McGriddle."

Berkeley started jumping up and down. "Can I get pancakes?"

"Of course you can, baby girl. You can have pancakes and orange juice and even sausage if you want."

Berkeley squealed. "Come on, Livy," and ran back into our bedroom.

I don't know why but I did not squeal or run back to the bedroom. Instead I watched Mom as she finished scrubbing.

She looked up at me. "Why aren't you getting ready?"

I wanted to tell her the stuff I told Melody.

About the hamburger.

About how school was horrible.

About how most of my teachers said I couldn't catch up.

I wanted to tell her that she ruined everything. And about why wasn't Dad emailing me back? Or writing me back? And about how nothing ever ends up good except for when I do my own thing—when she doesn't ruin it. Like I might get my hair reverse permed by Melody even if she didn't like it. Like I might move to Zimbabwe even if she said Africa was full of wild animals. Like I might get on a Greyhound and go find Dad even if Lala said he was trashy and had a girlfriend and even if Mom promised he'd come back because I had a feeling he never would.

I wanted to tell her all those things.

But then I said, "I don't feel like eating McDonald's."

This was a lie and she knew it was a lie. She sat back on her heels and looked at me.

"Is that so?"

"Yes."

"You don't want a Sausage Egg McMuffin?"

"No."

"You don't want orange juice?"

"Nope."

"You don't want an apple pie?"

I tried to keep my face normal even though sometimes I think about those pies at night.

"No, thank you."

She narrowed her eyes, which made her look like an evil lady and she said, taking off her gloves, "Fine by me. You going to go hang out with your best friend Melody?"

Mom and Berk had got home late the night before and she saw me sitting with Melody. Melody had shown me some of her tricks on her unicycle which she really was so good at and then she'd braided my hair into a fishtail which I like very much and when Mom got out of the car we were laughing and Mom said, "What's going on here?"

And Melody stood up and said, "Hey, LeAnn."

And Mom said, "Take Berkeley inside the house, Liv. It's time for dinner."

And I looked at Melody who was saying, "It's okay. We had a good time."

And Mom said, "It's not okay, Melody. She should've

been inside doing homework. Has she been out here long?" Mom was using a nasty voice and even though my mom is tired and can yell sometimes, she's not nasty.

I didn't get this. Whatever was going on, I didn't get it.

Why was she mean to Melody? Weren't they sort of the same in some ways? Both their husbands gone?

And now she was saying to me, "You going to hang out with your best friend Melody?"

I said, "Maybe."

And she said, "Fine by me."

She stood up. Even in her old sweats and Justin Bieber T-shirt from the thrift store, she looked nice. Not fancy like Melody but beautiful. Like someone who should be a good mom.

She used to be a good mom, I think.

But now . . .

"Berkeley," she yelled. "Let's go."

"Aren't you going to get dressed?" I asked her.

"I am dressed."

"You're going to wear that?"

"Yep."

I said, "Oh."

I guess I thought she'd take time to get ready like she always did and then we'd talk and she'd ask why I didn't want to go and then I'd say, "No. I don't want to tell you," and then she'd say, "I'm your mother. Please.

You can tell me anything," and then she'd beg me and then we'd hug and go eat Egg McMuffins and orange juice and apple in-my-mouth pie.

But instead she and my sister put on their shoes, held hands, and went out the door, Berkeley turning to look at me just as it shut.

I watched the Pontiac drive out of the neighborhood.

They left without me.

CHAPTER 39

I sat in the kitchen.

I sat in the front room.

I thought about writing Dad.

Or going to the library and emailing him.

I thought about not emailing him just to show him how it felt.

I thought about eating breakfast.

I didn't want to eat dumb-bum corn flakes again.

I sat in my room.

I wished I could enter some contests.

I looked at my face in the mirror and checked if any of my freckles had gone away.

Then I heard screams outside.

CHAPTER 40

I looked out the window and it was Carlene. She was screaming that Chip's monster truck was in flames! FLAMES!

I didn't know what to do but then I knew exactly what to do and I ran out the door in my nightgown, grabbed the neighborhood hose, and while Carlene and her stepmom and Lala and Bonnie and all of them were standing there bawling, and Chip, who was the most devastated of all of course, was rolling around in the dirt in a ball, wailing, "My baby! My baby," while all that, I started spraying the fire.

I even went right up to the heated truck that was crumbling before our very eyes, and sprayed and sprayed and sprayed and when most of the flames were out, Carlene was still crying: PEBBLES! PEBBLES! Which is the name of her cat, which I am allergic to, and she said, "He's in the cab! The cab!" and even though my body told me no, my heart told me yes.

People were all out of their trailers now.

Bob.

Grant.

Melody.

Mrs. Sydney Gunnerson.

Delilah.

Wanda and Jerry.

Baby George and his family.

Sadie and Jane.

Paul.

The black mamba owner.

The drug dealers.

Everyone was out, some cheering, some crying, others taking pictures.

So anyway, against the will of my body and even though I knew I might die, I climbed the wreckage and found the poor cat, huddled under the seat, meowing and meowing and for a brief second he said, "Olivia. I knew you'd come."

And I said, "I love you, Pebbles. I would never let you down."

And then I picked him up and ran him out to safety.

And that's when I saw something out my window.

It wasn't a monster truck on fire.

Instead it was Bart or Harrison or whatever his name was sitting on the trampoline.

He had a Mohawk.

CHAPTER 41

A Mohawk.

And he was here.

But I didn't care.

Because he ran away and he said he'd come back and then he didn't and he lied.

He *did* go to school.

He went to *my* school. Dixon Middle School.

Just like everyone else.

He wasn't like me and I wasn't like him so I didn't care.

I was just going to sit in my room and let him sunburn his face off out there for all I cared.

But then I looked again.

He was jumping and trying to do a trick, which looked really bad how he landed on his head.

I thought about it.

What if he left?

I wouldn't care.

But I might care.

Or what if Carlene went out there and talked to him?

And he became friends with her.

And what if Bonnie was there?

And Lala.

And what if he started going to the mall with them?

Not that that would happen. But what if it did? And what if he fell in love with Carlene or maybe even Bonnie but Carlene was more likely because Carlene was nice and had long eyelashes.

What if he fell in love with her and they got married and they moved into Carlene's trailer and had babies and Bart started driving monster trucks and nothing was ever the same again.

What if that?

I threw on some cutoffs.

I grabbed a T-shirt.

Put on some lip gloss and some turtle earrings and then I ran out the door before he could disappear again even though I didn't even care.

"Hey," I said, trying not to huff.

"Hey," he said. "I might not be able to stay long."

Like I cared how long he stayed.

So I turned to leave.

"Where are you going?" he said.

"Wherever I want," I said.

I started walking toward my trailer and I waited for him to say stop. Stop! Don't go!

At first he didn't and I started to feel panic in my heart but then he said, "Wait."

So I waited.

"I need your help," he said

I turned. "You need my help?" Beads of sweat were already forming on his forehead.

"Yeah," he said. "Sorry it's taken me so long to get back. Bureau crap."

"Bureau crap?"

"I don't know if I mentioned it but I work for the FBI. Long story. I'll have to tell you later," he said.

Ugh. But I decided to let it go.

"Where's the milk?"

"I drank it."

"You drank it?"

"The whole entire thing. On the way over."

I tried not to laugh. "You did not."

"I did. I was super thirsty."

I folded my arms very serious.

"You got a Mohawk," I said.

"Yep," he said.

"Do you like it?" I said.

"Do you like it?" he said.

I felt myself get warm but I said yes anyway.

He said, "I do too."

Then I said, "I saw you at school."

He stopped smiling. "No, you didn't."

"Yes, I did."

"I don't go to school."

"Yes, you do."

"What school?"

"Dixon."

"Dixon what?" he said.

"Dixon what?" I said.

"Yeah, Dixon what? I've never heard of it."

"You've never heard of it?"

"Nope."

More lies.

"You go to Dixon Middle School. You get free lunch because you work in the cafeteria."

That was a guess but it was the only thing I could figure out. I almost applied for free lunch when school first started but Mom wouldn't sign the paper because she said we didn't need anything for free and I said, "Yes, we do," and she gave me a big old lecture about not taking things that weren't ours.

But maybe if I could work in the cafeteria for lunch, it technically wouldn't be free? I'd have to look into it.

"Never heard of it." He shook his head. "I've heard of the Mason-Dixon Line, if that's what you're talking about." He took out a pencil and wrote something on a piece of paper that I don't know where he got.

Then he looked over at Grant and Bob's trailer.

I stared at him. His face was handsome. His skin looked soft and smooth and I wondered if he had ever been on an elephant. And also he was a liar.

But I said, "What's the Mason-Dixon Line?"

He looked at me. "You're kidding, right?"

My stomach started to rumble. I hated feeling stupid. Did he do this on purpose?

"Yeah," I said. "I'm kidding. Everyone knows that."

He said, "Oh yeah. Then what is it?"

"I'm not telling."

"You don't know."

"I do know but it doesn't matter because you're trying to distract me because I did see you at the lunchroom at Dixon Middle School."

"No, you didn't."

"Yes, I did."

And he said, "The Mason-Dixon Line was a cultural boundary between the North and the South for slavery even though it earlier was a line between the British colonies during a fight. But now it is still the state lines for Pennsylvania, Maryland, Delaware, and West Virginia."

He was talking fast and his face was a tomato.

Then he said, "Have you even been to Pennsylvania, Maryland, Delaware, or West Virginia?" He was practically yelling now, passionate is what my mom would call it.

I swallowed. He was smart. I was not so smart. I said, "No."

He took a deep long breath.

Then he said, "Neither have I."

CHAPTER 42

Bart and I sat there quiet.

I thought about how I had no idea who he was and how he had no idea who I was and yet I still felt like there was something holding us together.

Someone in the KOA Park turned on the radio and music started. Country music.

What if we started dancing?

What if he took my hand and pulled me up and I said, "What are you doing?" And he said, "What do you think I'm doing?" and then we slow danced on the tramp. Right there. On a crappy Saturday.

Bart looked at me. My heart fluttered.

Then he said, "But I want to go to all those places."

I said, "What places?"

And he said, "What?"

And I said, "What?"

And he said, "Those places. Pennsylvania, Delaware, Maryland, West Virginia."

I swallowed. "Me too. I want to go everywhere."

"You do?"

I said, "Yes."

He said, "Everywhere?"

I said, "Yeah, everywhere."

"Even Mongolia?"

I nodded. "Sure."

"It's cold."

"I don't care," I said, and he smiled.

Then I said, "Is your name Harrison?"

And he said, "That's my code name."

I said, "Oh."

And I said, "Is Bart your real name?"

And he said, "That's my FBI name."

"Your FBI name?"

And he said, "I told you it's a long story," and I said, "Ha-ha."

And he said, "Ha-ha" back.

And I said, "So you really are in the FBI?"

He said, "I can't say."

And even if he was lying, which he was, I thought maybe if he was in the FBI, he could help me find my dad. Or at least help me find out if he was trash. Or if he had a girlfriend.

But he was lying. So I said, "Shut up."

He said, "Okay."

And I said, "UGH." Then I said, "What's your real name?"

And he said, "If I told you, I'd have to kill you," which I hated.

So I said, "Will you be in our neighborhood circus?"

And he said, "Sure."

CHAPTER 43

Sometimes I wonder why things have to happen when they happen.

Like what if my mom and dad hadn't met in high school.

What if they'd met in China while they were both backpacking the Great Wall.

What if they'd met on a train to Cairo, my mom wearing huge sunglasses, my dad with a mustache.

Or what if they'd met on a plane to Moscow, where people were whispering and clinking wineglasses.

Or better yet, what if they'd met in a museum in Paris and fell in love in front of the *Mona Lisa*.

What if they didn't meet in PE at Provo High School where Mom was sitting with her friends on the gym floor talking and Dad was playing basketball and getting slammed into them and my mom had to go to the nurse and get stitches.

What if instead he saw her, and he knew. His blood running hot, his face red, and he knew.

Not because of no real reason but because she was

brilliant and witty and wrote articles for the *National Geographic* and used to live with a pride of lions.

And what if their first kiss wasn't in my dead grandma's stinky basement, with the cat litter and the patches of carpet covering the concrete floor.

What if they kissed on the Eiffel Tower or on a junk boat in Hong Kong or on the top of the Empire State Building or maybe even on the Mason-Dixon Line.

I sometimes wonder if everything would be different if my parents kissed somewhere better.

Somewhere real.

Bart, or whatever his name was, said, "Let's go on a bike ride."

The two of us sitting on the tramp talking about the Mason-Dixon Line and then how he could do tons of different things if we really did do a circus because he has a lot of skills like hoop dancing and plate spinning and he could swallow fire.

"No you can't."

"I can."

"You can't," I said, laughing.

"Really," he said, his face serious. "I've eaten tons of fire."

And I told him we probably wouldn't really do it but if

we did, we'd need him to, for sure, do something. "Like even be the announcer person," I said.

"The Master of Ceremony?" he said. "Easy." And I couldn't help it, I laughed again.

But then he said, "Let's go."

"Go where?"

He jumped up. Got off the tramp and pulled my dad's bike up that had been rotting in the weeds.

I flushed. Go on a bike ride?

"Whose is this?" he said.

"No one's."

"No one's?"

I wished I wasn't having this conversation.

He got on the bike.

"It probably has flat tires. It hasn't been ridden for a year," I said.

He put his foot on the pedal.

"I bet it's broken," I said.

"It's probably too big for you," I said.

"You won't want to ride it," I said.

And then he was pedaling onto the street, on my dad's bike.

I watched him weave along the one lane, one-way road. He rode out of sight, went all the way around the loop and then showed up again.

"It's a good bike," he said. And that was true. Mom and Dad had argued about it for a whole night when he'd brought it home. My dad had "impulse problems." I knew that much.

I didn't say anything.

"Where's yours?"

I shrugged. I hadn't ridden my bike for just as long as my dad's had been lying around. Bart popped a wheelie. Sort of. Actually he tried to and then he crashed and I said, "Oh my gosh," and he said, "I'm fine," and he jumped up and I said, "Are you okay?" And he said, "I'm fine," even though his knee was bleeding.

He got back on the bike.

I liked him.

"Where's yours?" he said again.

"Behind the house," I said.

"Go get it," he said.

"No."

"Why not?"

"I don't feel like it."

He put the bike down in the middle of the road. Jogged behind the trailer and I thought my heart was going to burst. I don't even know why.

"It has a flat," he yelled.

"Oh," I said.

"There's a pump here."

I stared at the sky. "There is?" I said.

"Yeah."

Then he came riding out on my bike.

"Come on," he said. He set down the bike and got on Dad's.

"I thought you couldn't stay long."

"I'm supposed to go somewhere but I don't care," he said.

I felt shaky and nervous and I said, "Really?" and he said, "Come on."

And right at that moment, my whole body said, "Please God, don't let it start like this."

I hadn't been on my bike.

I wasn't going to ever go on my bike.

Not until Dad got back.

But Bart was riding around waiting for me. Smiling.

And I said, "No God. Please no. Don't let him be the one that I fall in love with."

Don't let him be the one.

I felt a tear start to form.

I was wearing a stained T-shirt with flowers and a hole in the side.

He had on those baggy torn-up jeans.

We were in our stupid trailer park where no one's lives ever worked out.

The sky wasn't blue. It was filled with clouds.

Mom and Berkeley were eating McGriddles without me.

And I was sweating.

Please. Not like this.

Because I liked him.

And what if he liked me.

Please God. Let me not love him.

I didn't want to meet and fall in love with the love of
my life now. Not here. Not like this.

But then he was biking to the jogging path.

And right then I had a choice.

I could stop this.

I could sit here.

I could let him leave.

I could go inside.

I could make Nestlé milk.

I could lie in bed.

I could call the police and say a bike was stolen.

I could walk to McDonald's and tell Mom I was sorry.

I could go to the library and email Dad and enter
forty-five thousand more contests.

I could find Carlene and ask about Monster Jam.

I could sit with Melody and eat her cookies and get a
reverse perm.

I could do so many many things.

I had a choice and once again the teeny tiny barely-there voice in the little pocket in my stomach whispered, "Go."

And I whispered, "I can't."

And it whispered, "Be brave."

And I said, "Is this brave?"

And it said, "Be brave."

And that was it because I didn't know what being brave was but that voice did, I hoped.

"Wait," I yelled, and I jumped off the tramp and got on my bike and then did things I never do.

CHAPTER 44

I did things like I went out of the gate and followed a boy named Bart or whoever he was on the trail and he was riding fast so I was riding fast even though usually I'm careful and I don't want to crash and my heart was thumping and my hair was flying and people were looking and Bart was laughing and I was laughing, too.

I was laughing.

I did things like ride along the river and almost hit a family with bike helmets and knee pads and the dad yelled, "Watch where you're going!" And Bart yelled, "Sorry!" And I yelled, "Sorry!" but I didn't look back.

I did things like follow Bart to a spot in the trees and stop and throw rocks in the water and try to hit the old canoe on the other bank and Bart missed so bad and I hit it right on. And he said, "Whoa," and I said, "That was easy."

And then he looked at me one second too long like we were in a movie. Him with a Mohawk, me with a-a-a-a nothing. But it didn't matter.

I did things like listen to Bart when he told me that his cousin once drank the water in the river and he got cholera and had to be in a hyperbaric chamber for months and I said, "You can't get cholera from the Provo River," and he said, "You can and he did," and I said, "Is he okay?" and he said, "He sells used cars, so no, he's not okay."

I did things like go with him, go with him all the way to the end of the trail, just the two of us. And then watched as he kept going, off the paved trail onto the gravel toward the beach and I yelled, "What are you doing!" and he kept riding, right into the water of Utah Lake. Right into the crystal clear blue water until he was up to his knees and then up to his chest and then he kept on going until he disappeared, his whole body, everything, buried down down down into the deep and should I follow him?

Do I follow you Bart?

"Be brave," said the whisper. "Be brave."

And so I did.

I rode right on into the water like it was nothing.

And he was waiting for me.

He and me, under the water where the fish said, "Hi," and a gigantic purple octopus had set up a table and chairs and there was a Big Mac for him and an apple pie for me and he said, "I've never brought anyone here before."

And I said, "I've never been brought anywhere before."

And he said, "I love you."

And I said, "Don't love me."

And he said, "Why not?"

And I said, "Please don't."

And he said, "I can't help it."

And I thought maybe he couldn't. I thought maybe there was nothing I could do to stop it because I thought maybe I loved him, too. And maybe there would never be another him and another me that went together so well in the whole universe.

Is that how it happened, Dad? Is that how it happened, Mom? You couldn't help yourself?

You couldn't help yourself?

And if that's true, why can they help themselves now?

CHAPTER 45

Except really, we sat on the bank of Utah Lake.

Our crappy bikes lying in the dirt.

The water wasn't clear. It was muddy and brown.

There were loud WaveRunners and it stunk like garbage and Bart said, "Sometimes I think things in my head are going to be one way and then they turn out to be completely different."

I looked at him.

He had his chin on his knees.

I said, "How?"

He sat there.

I waited.

And waited.

Then he looked at me.

And he said, "I'm supposed to be at my dad's."

"What?"

"It's my dad's weekend," he said.

A WaveRunner went by spraying water so close to us I could almost feel it on my face.

"Where does he live?" I asked.

"In some condos by the train station," he said.

Then I said, "Oh."

Then he said, "I hate going there."

I was quiet because I didn't know what to say. But then I said, "Is he mean?"

Bart shook his head. "No."

"No?"

"No."

"Then why do you hate it there?"

"I don't know," he said. "It's boring."

We sat there. It was hot.

I said, "They're divorced?"

He nodded. "Yep."

"How long?"

He shrugged. "Since I was six."

"Six," I said. Berkeley was five.

"Yep," he said.

Then we sat.

"Is it bad?"

He looked at me. "Is what bad?"

"Them being divorced?"

"It's fine," he said.

It's fine, I thought.

Then he said, "Are yours divorced?"

A big fat lump got in my throat.

"No."

"Oh," he said.

Then I said, "But my dad's gone."

He looked at me. "Where is he?"

I looked at my hands. "I think Bryce Canyon."

He said, "Bryce Canyon? I've been there."

"You have?" And I was about to ask if he'd seen him or if he thought maybe park rangers didn't get internet or if Bryce Canyon had girlfriends there but instead I said, "They're not divorced. He's just on a break. He needed a break."

I waited for him to say that was stupid. That my dad was never coming back. That they pretty much were divorced.

I waited.

And waited.

But then he said, "Do you know how to swim?"

CHAPTER 46

When we got back, our clothes were almost dry because we rode so fast, and my mouth was aching because I'd been laughing and laughing and laughing. We dropped our bikes and then I saw our car, which meant Mom and Berk were back and I wanted to bring Bart inside.

I wanted Mom to meet him.

I wanted to say, "Mom, this is my friend, Bart."

I was about to invite him in, maybe tell him he could stay for tuna fish sandwiches or maybe we could even get Little Caesars pizza, I was about to do all that when Bart whispered hard, "Get down, get down." He pulled me to the grass, hiding behind Mom's car parked badly on the patch of lawn.

"What's wrong?" I looked around. There was no screaming. No fights. No cop cars. No fireworks. Nothing.

Just the sounds of a softball game. The pinwheels in Delilah's yard spinning. Tandi's herb garden putting off the smell of mint. The park actually looked pretty, I thought.

The only person outside was Grant on his beach chair.

Bart said, "Don't let him see us."

"Who?"

"Him," he said.

I looked over at Grant. "Grant?"

"Yeah. Grant."

Grant burped. His bare belly jiggling.

"Why can't he see us?"

And he said, "Because. FBI."

And I said, "What?"

And he said, "FBI."

And I said, "Really?"

While we were swimming he told me that something was going on in my neighborhood. That he was doing surveillance. I could see there being concern about the Conways or that motorcycle guy or even that Mrs. Sydney Gunnerson could be smuggling in those dolls. But Grant? Why would anyone care about Grant's dumb-bum life?

But clearly Bart did.

We watched Grant put grease all over his fat belly, drink Mountain Dew, and sing *We Built this City on Rock an' Roll.*

And then we saw Melody. She wasn't on the steps anymore. She was moving boxes or something around the outside of her trailer and Grant said, "Melody. Go get me another Dew."

And she said, "What?" And he said, "Get me a Dew." He pointed to a box that was by his door.

And she said, "Get your own Dew, butthead."

And Bart whispered, "I like her."

And I said, "I like her, too."

And then we watched Grant sit there and sit there and sit there and finally I said, "Are we going to do this much longer because my back hurts?" and Bart said, "Shhhhh," and we had to keep lying there but thankfully Bob got back soon and he and Grant got in a fight because Grant left work early and wasn't supposed to be lying around and he kept staying out late at night and not turning off the lights when he got in and then they started arguing about a football team and then they went inside.

That's when we finally sat up.

"If you're really watching Grant, he's not a criminal."

"How do you know?" he asked.

"Because he doesn't do anything. He just sits around. Eats. Drinks. Goes to work."

"That guy said he goes out at night."

I shrugged. "So?"

"So. That's when he does bad things."

I thought about how much I knew Grant. He'd been here for as long as I could remember. He sometimes helped Mom fix her car radio or gave us leftover headphones from his store that were sort of broken. He liked to play catch with a football whenever anyone would do it with him because he used to play in high school and he was a big star according to him, and at Halloween he always dressed up as Frankenstein and gave out king-sized candy bars.

One time he'd had a girlfriend named Trinity, the only time I'd ever remembered him having someone, and she had lots of tattoos and thick dark sunglasses that she always wore and she was nice because she said, "You girls want some gum?" It was Hubba Bubba Grape.

She gave us each two pieces.

Grant said to her, "These girls are sort of like daughters to me," and I looked at him because we weren't like daughters at all but he was smiling and so then I thought I'd smile, too, because everyone deserves to get a chance at love.

And Trinity said, "Aren't you the sweetest," and Grant said, "I really am the sweetest," and they started rubbing noses and I said, "Gross," but not out loud.

She ended up dumping him for a man named Mickey and everyone knew because Grant cried and cried and cried and told everyone and couldn't think straight and Mom gave him peppermint tea back then and Dad said, "Dude, you got to pull it together. A woman is not worth this kind of torment," and he said, "I know, I know but we were together two months, you know? I thought this was going somewhere," and Bob said to Dad that Grant was a big fat baby.

So Grant, though a big fat baby and everything, was nice for the most part. He didn't seem like he'd do anything illegal.

Bart disagreed. "He's into some things that could hurt a lot of people."

I stared at him. "Really?"

"Really."

"What about Bob?"

"What?"

"Bob. I would think Bob would be the one who would be more of a threat. He's smarter."

"Who?"

"Bob. His brother."

Bart thought about this for a minute, which was strange because why wouldn't he know about Grant's brother? Like if there was an FBI case, surely Bob would have his own folder.

"Who's older?" he asked.

"Uhh." I had no idea. "I think maybe Grant?"

"It kind of seemed like the other guy was older."

"That's because Grant is lazy but more fun."

"Is he more fun? How is he fun?"

This was weird. "Why do you care? How do you know him?"

Bart got professional all of a sudden. "He has a file at the FBI a mile high. He's a dangerous person and he could possibly be a part of a gang."

I started laughing. "A gang?"

"Yeah," Bart said. "Why is that so funny?"

"Because he just lies around."

"So."

"So he's like a teddy bear."

Bart didn't seem satisfied. He stared over at the trailer.

"Can you start documenting details about Grant?"

"Details?"

He wanted me to make a list of facts I knew about Grant.

"Like everything."

He also wanted me to write down when Grant left and came home every day. He wanted me to write down who came and went from his trailer. He told me to keep track of anything suspicious and how many beers he drank.

"How many beers? How do I do that?"

Just count the boxes.

And it was true; Bob and Grant always had a growing mound of Budweiser boxes outside their place that were taken away by the garbage guy each week.

"Bob drinks, too," I said.

Bart said, "Just count the boxes."

"Okay," I said.

"Okay," he said.

He stood up to leave.

I stood up, too.

"Will I see you at the lunchroom?" I asked. I hoped that maybe since today happened, he'd stop pretending he didn't go to Dixon. We could walk together at school. He could maybe get me a job in the cafeteria, too. We could stand around together at fifteen-minute break. Maybe we could even hold hands someday.

He looked at me for a long time and I looked at him for a long time and he said, "Sure."

My heart soared like a rocket.

Before he left he gave me his email address and I said thanks and I didn't tell him that the computer was broken because I could just go to the library and he said you're welcome and then he left and he kissed me but he didn't but if he had I would have kissed him back and then I would have done a cartwheel and I wouldn't have cared that he saw or anyone else.

CHAPTER 47

I almost skipped up the stairs to our trailer but then, when I went inside, everything changed.

Mom had tears on her face. "Where the hell in nations have you been?"

My stomach dropped. "I went for a bike ride."

I looked over. Berkeley was huddled in the corner.

"You went for a bike ride? What are you talking about?"

The air was tight and I tried to take a breath.

I knew she was saying that because I hadn't been on my bike for so long she'd probably forgotten I knew how to ride.

I said, "I'm sorry."

And she said, "Sorry? Sorry? Why didn't you leave a note?"

That would have been a good idea. In fact, that was what I normally would have done at least for Berkeley's sake. I was the one who was responsible. The one who did the right thing. How long had I been gone?

I didn't think they'd care but I realized it must have been hours.

She said, "You smell awful."

"I was in the lake," I said.

"In the lake? Swimming?"

I smiled even though I didn't want to because it had been funny and we'd floated for hours and I'd never realized how beautiful that dumb-bum dirty lake actually was. No one went swimming there because they said it was too polluted. Shows what they know.

"Yeah," I said. "Swimming."

She looked shocked and I liked it. Maybe I wasn't who she thought I was. Just like she wasn't who I thought she was.

"Who were you with?"

I was about to say Bart, my friend. My best friend. A boy.

I was about to say I was with one of the best people I know but then I got scared.

What if she said I couldn't hang out with him?

She didn't want me talking to Melody.

She told me to stay away from Earl Bowen or any of the renter trailers.

What if she didn't want me talking to Bart?

"No one," I said.

She stared at me and I stared at her and I waited for her to do something. Yell at me or slap me or say I know you were with Bart Harrison and you can never see him again.

But then she just deflated, like an old balloon.

"I got the computer fixed," she said.

"You what?"

"It was a surprise. You didn't even notice it was gone."

I looked over. There it sat. Like it had for over a week. But now it had a sticker on it that said GEEKSQUAD.

"McDonald's and computer guys," she said.

"Oh," I said. I tried to swallow but it was hard. She got my computer fixed. I wanted to ask how much it cost. Maybe I could pay her back someday. I wanted to say I was so sorry but she had already turned and walked back to her room.

I went over to Berkeley who hadn't said a word and I went over there and she was shaking. Hard.

I was sorry.

Really really really sorry.

Sometimes people do stupid things. Stupid things to people for stupid reasons.

I'd done something stupid to my sister.

I whispered it into her ear. "I won't ever leave you again."

She looked at me. "I didn't know where you were."

I nodded. "I know."

"I didn't know if you were coming back."

"I know," I said. Then I said, "I'll always come back."

"You promise?" she asked.

And I said, "I promise."

She picked up her doll. Held it.

Then she said, "We got you an apple pie."

CHAPTER 48

My mom and dad used to take Berk and me biking on the river trail.

Like we were normal people.

Like we didn't actually LIVE on the trail, but we were a family that had a house and chickens and a dog and maybe a playground all our own and we rode our bikes because we liked the sound of the river and the peacefulness of the trees and not because it was how we got home from school or how we got to the grocery store.

And we said hi to people, especially Dad who knew just about every person everywhere he went, and Mom would laugh and you could tell she loved him and loved that he was so popular and funny. And then we stopped and ate peanut butter and jelly sandwiches and real carrot sticks that Mom had peeled and cut, and once we even had lemonade.

I think about that and I wonder if he thinks about it.

I wonder if he misses it.

One time I asked Mom if we could go on a ride after he left and she said, "Go ahead."

And I said, "Can you come, too?"

And she said, "I'm exhausted."

I sat next to her on the couch. She smelled like cleaning solution and her hands looked old. Way older than she was.

"What about tomorrow?" I asked.

"I have to work."

"What about on your day off?"

"I have to run errands and Judy wants me to come over and do her house."

"You're cleaning Judy's house?"

Judy was one of my mom's friends from high school.

Mom laid her head on the back of the couch and closed her eyes. "She's paying me double, so yeah."

"Can I come help?"

She opened one eye. "You want to help me?"

"Yeah," I said. "I do."

And I suddenly really did. Really.

She closed the eye again. "Nah. You need to stay here and watch Berk."

I laid my head on the couch, too. I was tempted to ask if me *and* Berk could come but I already knew Judy wouldn't like that.

I watched as she sat there, or slept there, whatever she was doing, her chest going in and out and in and out.

She was so little. Like a bird. And some days she looked like she was going to break. Or get shot out of the sky and fall down dead.

I never asked her to go biking again.

CHAPTER 49

Sunday night I emailed Bart on our brand-new fixed computer.

....

Dear Bart,

   I don't know if you are in the FBI.

   But if it helps, I saw Grant outside again today.

   It's out of his normal routine because he was wearing jogging shorts and no shirt and looked like he was going to try to exercise or something, which he's never done in his whole entire life. He went on the jogging trail but was back in ten minutes.

   Please instruct.

                                    From, Olivia

   P.S. Are you really running in a hundred-mile race? Which race?

....

Two minutes later he emailed back.

....

Olivia:

Please focus on his emotional state. Particularly after coming home from events. We are concerned he is unbalanced and a danger to society.

Please don't use his real name.

From now on, he will go by Gandalf. I am deleting your previous email to erase evidence even though anything you do on your computer is never gone so really you have compromised this investigation but I will discuss this with my superiors and see if they will let it slide.

Also, my entire room smells like dead fish.

Sincerely,

B.

P.S. I am running in the Wasatch Back. It is on August 20. If you would like to bring me water, I would very much appreciate it.

....

I wrote back.

....

Bart.

I will watch Gandalf very carefully but I would like some spy gear to help.

Also, will there ever be a time I will get more details about this mission?

My whole house also smells like fish. And I'm grounded.

Cordially,
Olivia

P.S. I would like to run in the race. Not give you water.

....

Dear Olivia,

I'll tell you more when you have proven yourself.

I can't use email during weekdays sometimes because of FBI policy so we'll have to just communicate face-to-face at school. Let's meet at the drinking fountain by the lunchroom.

Also, I just found out that on PBS they are doing shows on the most famous circuses in the world beginning Monday night starting with the New Shanghai Circus, which is clearly the best circus of all of them.

You and Berk should watch to get ideas. I can do any of the acts probably.

Masterfully,
B

....

Dear Bart,

I thought you don't watch TV.

Regrettably,
Olivia

....

Dear Olivia,

I don't and you shouldn't either.

Professionally,
B

....

I laughed.
I looked up Wasatch Back on the computer.
August 20.
I put it on the calendar.

Then I emailed Dad.

....

Dear Dad,

It turns out Bart is not a liar. I spent the whole afternoon with him and he can pop wheelies and we went swimming and he told me some top-secret things.

I can't talk about a lot of it because he's on some kind of secret military spy mission that is being overseen by the FBI. He said Grant is under surveillance. I told him you might be doing some of that too because you work for the National Park Service and he said that the National Park Service has nothing to do with national security and we got in an argument about that. Do you have anything to do with the FBI?

He said he'd want to meet you. I said he should come to Las Vegas to the Monster Truck show. He said he'd ask his mom.

I stopped writing. I thought about saying this: Are you and Mom divorced?

I also thought about writing this: Do you love her anymore?

I also also thought about writing this: Do you love someone else? How does love work?

And then I thought about writing this: I may be in love with someone.

Instead I wrote,

    That's all.

                  Love, Liv

....

On Monday morning, I was excited about school for the first time. I tried on five different outfits. I did my hair in a semi-fishtail, sort of, but then took it out because it looked bad but who cares and got all my homework packed in order of my classes.

I woke Berk up.

I woke Mom up.

I got cereal for everyone.

So excited.

But then

Mom's cell rang. It was 7:25 in the morning.

We all looked at each other.

"I don't know the number," she said.

"Maybe it's Dad," Berk said.

Mom and I looked at her. Berk never talked about Dad. I'd almost thought she'd forgotten about him.

"It's not Dad," Mom said.

Mom answered it.

Berk and I watched as she listened to the voice on the other end.

"What are you talking about?" she said.

She stood up.

"What? She would never do that." She walked over to the window. Glanced at Berkeley.

"I have nowhere else to take her. Why didn't you tell me over the weekend?"

I looked at Berkeley who was not looking at me or Mom. Rather she was shoveling Cheerios in her mouth and maybe, just maybe, trying not to smile.

Finally, Mom got off the phone.

She walked over to Berk. Sat down.

"Berkeley?"

Berk took another bite. Still not looking at Mom.

"Berkeley. Did you take something at day care?"

I looked at Mom. Shocked. "What are you talking about?"

Mom ignored me. Stared at Berk.

"She said you took some money out of one of the worker's purse."

Berkeley was chewing. And chewing and chewing. Finally, each word taking forever to get out of her mouth, she said, "I put it back."

"You put it back?"

"I put it back."

Mom looked at me. I was just as surprised as her.

"She says you can't come back."

"Oh," Berk said.

"And she said that she might call the police."

"Okay," Berkeley said. She reached for more milk.

"Did you hear me, miss? You could go to jail."

Berkeley nodded. She was so calm.

She wasn't going to jail. We all knew that.

Mom stood there. I thought she might yell at Berk. Or at me. Or at someone.

But then she just sat down. She was too tired to yell, I guess. "What am I going to do now?"

"Can't you find another place?" I asked.

She looked at her hands.

"Mom. There are a lot of day cares."

She shook her head. "I couldn't even afford that place. I have to be at work in fifteen minutes. I don't have time for this."

We all sat quiet.

"Why can't I just stay home?" she said. "Livy can take care of me."

I looked at her. She smiled at me and I realized, she planned this. She planned it. She thought she could stay home if she got kicked out of day care. She probably thought I would get to stay home, too.

She *was* smart.

Mom looked at her. "Livy can't stay home. She has to go to school."

"What about Delilah?" I asked.

"She has work," Mom said.

"Maybe she could stay home."

Mom looked irritated. "I'm not going to ask someone to miss work for us, Olivia."

I nodded.

Then I said, "Melody doesn't have a job."

Mom's eyes narrowed. "No."

"Why not? She's really nice."

"No," Mom said again.

I didn't understand why Melody made Mom so mad. All she did was make cookies and sit on her dumb step and tell me she'd reverse perm my hair. Had they had a fight or something? Had Melody done something wrong?

Mom rubbed her forehead. "What am I going to do? What am I going to do?"

She glanced at Berkeley. "Do you think you could take care of yourself?" Mom said.

Was she serious?

Berk perked up.

"Mom. She's five," I said.

Mom shot me a look.

She knew I was right. You can't leave a five-year-old home alone, especially not where we lived.

But I'd made her mad. I could feel that I'd made her mad.

"I can't take her to work. Dennis would go through the roof," Mom said.

I thought about my mom's boss going through the roof and he was bald with round cheeks and I thought it would probably hurt and he'd bleed a lot.

"There's that one free preschool," I said.

Some lady had brought over a flyer for a head start place that was free for people who didn't have very much money.

She'd knocked on the door and Mom had stood on the stoop. "What makes you think we can't afford a regular preschool?" Mom asked, holding the pamphlet up to shade her eyes from the sun.

The lady was really nice. You could tell because she was wearing Bermuda shorts with white socks and she had frizzy hair and when Mom got after her, she turned red and got all fidgety. She probably was just out of college and trying to save people like me and Mom and Berk. Trying to make our lives better. I wished Mom would let her alone. Sometimes she doesn't let people alone.

"I'm sure you could afford it," the woman said.

"Oh really? You think we have enough money?" Mom said back.

The lady looked at me and I tried to give her a nice smile. A smile like, "It's okay. We probably don't have enough money." She looked back at Mom who said, "If you think we have enough money, why did you bring this here? Who sent you?"

"Oh," the lady said, smoothing her hair. "No one sent me. I mean, I'm taking the flyers everywhere."

"Everywhere?"

"Everywhere."

"Are you taking them to the houses on the hill?"

"Absolutely."

Mom stared at her and then the lady said, "I actually have to keep going. I hope you fine women have a fine day," and Mom said, "Fine women? Fine day? Who talks like that?"

But the lady was already walking away.

I looked at Mom.

"Why'd you have to do that?" I'd asked her.

"Do what?"

"You know what."

"I have no idea," Mom said. "Plus we don't need some stupid government preschool."

"We don't?" I asked.

"We don't," she said.

And that was that.

Until now.

Now we needed some stupid government preschool. We needed something.

She looked at me. "Do you think you could take her to school with you?"

I stared at her.

She stared back at me.

Not laughing.

Not saying, "Just kidding."

Just sitting there with her Diet Coke and her makeup.

She wanted me to take my baby sister to school with me. To my classes. To lunch. To fifteen-minute break.

"I'll just stay home," I said.

She closed her eyes and blew out a big burst of air. "I'll take care of it," she said.

She got up, grabbed her mug, and walked over and slammed it in the sink.

She stood there, her shoulders slumped and then, this really happened, she started to tremble. Like a leaf.

Just watching her made the whole room shrink.

I had to do something.

I had to fix this.

I said, "I guess I can take her to school with me."

Mom shook her head. "No, you can't."

"Yeah," I said. "It's okay. It'll be okay."

Mom looked at me. "I don't think it's allowed, is it?"

She was asking me like I knew the answer to that question and she didn't, even though I was pretty sure we both knew that no way was it okay for me to take my five-year-old sister with me to middle school. No way.

But I said, "It's fine. People do it all the time."

It was stupid.

It didn't even make sense.

There was no way.

No way.

But then she nodded. She nodded. And said, "Just for today."

Just for today.

Just for today.

"You can try it out and see how it goes," she said.

Then I was nodding, too, hard to find any words.

She smiled. "Thank you, Olivia. I can always count on you."

CHAPTER 51

Steve Fossett climbed almost all of the world's tallest mountains.

He climbed the Matterhorn in Switzerland and Mount Kilimanjaro in Tanzania, which is where the world's oldest skull was found.

He swam the English Channel and was in a dog sled race and an all-day and all-night car race.

He also never had kids.

You can do a lot of things if you don't have kids.

CHAPTER 52

I didn't know very much about Dixon.

I didn't know where the good closets were.

I didn't know if there was a basement where they stored old desks and textbooks.

I didn't know if there were offices that had mice or something bad so they kept them empty.

Basically, because I'd missed so much school I knew nothing useful about middle school.

When Mom dropped us off, this time me holding Berkeley's hand, she said, "I'll take you guys to the pool this week, okay?"

Berkeley said, "Yay!"

And I said, "Okay."

Then she said, "Walk home."

I nodded.

She winked at me. "Love you, Bumblebee," she said, like I was four years old again.

Love you.

Then she looked at Berkeley, "Love you too, Missy. Be good to your sister."

I started to tear up. Please don't go, I wanted to say. Even more than before. Please.

Then she drove away.

Just like that.

Just drove away.

I took a deep breath.

The thing was, it wasn't her fault.

I said I'd do it. *Me.*

This was *my* problem.

I'd said it.

She agreed to it.

Berkeley was bouncing. She'd never been to school before. Would there be tests?

"No."

"Will they do art?"

"No."

"Story time?"

I shook my head. How was I going to make this work? We could just go home but what if Mom found out? What if she really had to go to court and to jail?

We stood there, alone, with hundreds of kids my age getting out of cars and unloading off buses and locking up bikes. Talking in groups and throwing things.

I saw Carlene and dumb-bum Bonnie and I didn't want them to see Berkeley even though they knew her and maybe they would feel bad for me and help?

No. No. They wouldn't.

I scanned the crowds for Bart.

I thought he would help. He would. But then, what if he really *was* FBI? If he was, and if he saw us, he'd have to turn us in. Me in. Mom in. Dad in. Berk.

The voice in my gut started rumbling again. Rumbling and rumbling and it said: Take care of your sister.

Take care of your sister.

Take care of your sister.

Take care of your sister.

So I did.

I forgot about Bart. I forgot about Carlene and dumb-bum Bonnie. I even forgot about Mom and Dad and I took care of my sister.

I said, "Do what I say, Berk. And don't let go of my hand."

Then I took a deep breath, shook my hair out, which I wished was already reverse permed, and walked with my little sister right into Dixon Middle School.

CHAPTER 53

I once found out about a fish that if you rubbed it on your skin, you would fall down on the ground and die but you really wouldn't be dead.

You would appear dead.

Your pulse would be nothing.

Your heart would be nothing.

Your breathing would be nothing.

But you'd be alive.

Everything slowed down so much that they'd all bawl for you and they'd have to prepare a funeral for you.

And your body would lie on the bed and people would talk about the nice things you did. And how you saved their lives.

And how you won more contests than any other living person in the world.

And how you became an explorer.

And how you and your father were reunited and how he was held as a hostage for a time and that's why he couldn't communicate with you but you figured it out and you were able to find him when he was in a cave surrounded by deadly scorpions that were unusually large because of a genetic mutation and you battled them and you set him free.

And how he wasn't trashy at all.

And how he didn't have a girlfriend.

And how he'd been waiting for you, waiting and waiting.

They'd talk about all these things and your little sister would be sad and she would be hugging her doll that has no hair and Carlene and Lala and even Bonnie would be sobbing all over the place.

And Bart.

Bart would be there. And he'd be holding a tuna fish sandwich with Doritos and his eyes would be wet but he wouldn't cry. Not then. He had to be strong.

But most of all, your mom. Your mom would say, "I could always count on her. My Olivia. I could always count on her."

And then, when they were all so sad they could barely speak, you would cough.

Your dead body letting out a quiet peaceful cough.

Just one itty-bitty cough.

The entire room would freeze.

Could it be?

Then you'd cough again. A little louder.

Your dad would yell, "Olivia! Olivia!" And he'd run to your side.

And your mom would say, "Keith, is it true?"

And he'd turn and there would be tears streaming down his face and he'd say, "Yes! She's here! She's here! Our child is alive! She's alive!"

And then you'd sit up and everyone would shout and cry and hug each other.

And Mr. Brown would not be saying Olivia, "Do you know the answer to the question?"

I looked at him.

I looked at the clock behind his big head. It was 10:13. In the morning. I was in pre-algebra. I was in pre-algebra. He was asking me a question.

Berkeley was here.

She was in the supply closet we found upstairs.

In seven minutes I could check on her.

I'd already checked on her once and she was doing her coloring book.

"Olivia? Is something wrong?"

Someone whispered, "Retard."

And people laughed. Mr. Brown said, "Jared. Stay after class."

Then Mr. Brown said, "Are you okay?"

And I said, "I just have a headache."

And then he folded his arms and said, "You stay after class, too."

And Jared or whoever he was said, "BUUURRRRRN."
Which it was not a burn.

And then you sit there.

And you think, I wish the fish didn't work and I wish I was dead.

Mr. Brown talked to Jared first while I sat at my desk.

He said, "Do you think it's appropriate to ever use that word."

Jared said, "Yes."

Mr. Brown said, "Yes?"

And he said, "No."

"That's right. No. It's not appropriate. Ever. What do you have to say to Ms. Hales?"

Jared, who I'd never even seen before, looked at me. Then he said, "Sorry," and when Mr. Brown turned to look at me Jared made a pig face.

I looked at my desk.

"Do you accept his apology, Olivia?"

"Yes," I said.

He looked at Jared, who was now folding his arms and looked very concerned.

"Please don't ever let me hear you using that word ever again."

"Okay," said Jared. Then he said, "Can I have a pass?"

And Mr. Brown said, "No."

"No?"

"No."

"I'll get a tardy."

"Not my problem."

Jared glared at me. Then he grabbed his bag and walked out the door.

The bell rang which meant my next class was already starting which meant I wasn't going to get to check on Berkeley which meant she was going to be scared and what if she had to go to the bathroom and I had some crackers in my bag that I'd forgotten to leave with her and what if they'd found her because what if they used that closet even though it looked dusty and smelled like old rags and was clear out of the way but even though that, what if they found her?

Mr. Brown sat in the desk next to me. He smelled like my dad's spice shaving cream but he was about fifty years old and had rings of sweat under his arms.

"I'll give you a pass. Don't worry."

I said, "Okay."

"First of all, I'm sorry about what Jared said. People can be jerks."

I said, "Okay."

Then he said, "Second of all, I've been meaning to talk to you about what's been happening. We, your teachers, have met with your mom a few times and she told us you've been sick."

He'd met with my mom? When? And what was he talking about? I'd been sick?

He was watching me.

Was I sick?

Was this something Mom hadn't told me? Or Dad? Maybe that's why he left. Maybe he couldn't take it. Maybe I was dying. Was I dying? Or was this just something she told them so she wouldn't have to go to court.

Right then I felt sick to my stomach for real. If she'd told them that, things were getting really bad.

He was staring at me still. A sweat ball starting on his forehead.

I said, "Yes. Very sick."

He paused for a minute. Then he said, "How are you feeling now?"

"Better," I said. "A little better."

He kept staring, like he was studying me to see if I was telling the truth, which I was not.

"Did you get the note that you may have to go to summer school?"

I nodded. "Miss Hill gave it to me."

Miss Hill is a school counselor who told me she was my friend.

"Did your mother mention that?"

"Mention what?"

"Summer school."

"No."

"No?"

"No. Just Miss Hill."

"Huh," he said.

Then he said, "Did Miss Hill talk to you about your illness?"

I said, "No."

The counselor and this dumb-bum teacher. Had Mom told the principal I was sick? Who else had she told? I started to feel itchy.

I'd read an article about a mom who lied and told everyone her kid had cancer and got a whole bunch of money and then ended up in prison.

Prison.

Had my mom told them I had cancer?

He kept talking and I tried to focus. "Your mom said you were sensitive about it. How it was contagious. She really didn't want us discussing it with you now that you're on the mend."

"Okay," I said, feeling woozy.

"I want you to know that I've had some medical issues." He coughed. "That were not pretty."

I looked at my hands.

"I didn't want to talk about it either," he said.

He waited.

I said, "Thank you?"

And he said, "You're welcome."

Then he said, "If you can stay on task and get some help, I think you can catch up in this class before the end of the year. You're very smart."

I looked at him. I wasn't sure he knew who I was. Maybe he thought I was someone else.

"Do you still have that headache?"

I nodded.

He wrote me a pass and said, "Go to the nurse for now and get some medicine. I'll try to find you a tutor so you can catch up."

I said, "Okay."

And that was it.

Things were much worse than I thought and my mom might be going to prison.

CHAPTER 54

Berkeley was still in the closet.

She had made a pile of rectangles with her scissors.

"Tickets," she said. "For the circus."

I smiled. "That's good."

I took her to the bathroom in the upstairs one and luckily it was still during class so no one saw us.

"Are you okay?" I asked her once we were back.

"Yeah," she said. "I guess."

"Remember, this is a secret school. No one can know you're here."

"I remember," she said. "It's okay. I'll be okay."

She said it in a way that showed she understood, which was sad.

I handed her a notebook from math. "You can draw ideas on here for what we should have for the food and maybe for what we should wear."

She looked at me. "How long will it be until we can go home?"

I took a breath. "I have one more class and then I'll come in here and we'll eat lunch. Then it won't be long."

"Okay," she said, and I loved her. I loved her so so much.

~

I didn't meet Bart at the drinking fountain by the cafeteria.

I didn't look for him in the halls.

I didn't even hope he'd see me and take me with him to Mongolia.

Mostly I just kept my head down and tried to not get noticed.

On the walk home, Berkeley talked about trapezes and how to make them and about how school was kind of fun and how she wanted to get a new leotard and how I should probably wear one and I was thinking how this wasn't going to work.

Something had to happen: take care of your sister.

Take care of your sister.

Take care of your sister.

Something had to happen soon or everything was going to blow up and nothing would ever be the same again.

CHAPTER 55

One thing: Maybe Berk was only coming to school for one day.

Mom would figure something else out.

Find a day care.

Let Berk stay with a friend or Melody or Delilah.

And I could meet Bart at the lunchroom.

When we got home I helped Berk get into her old leotard which yes, she needed a new one, so she and Sadie and Jane could practice their circus acts outside.

I did my homework.

I cleaned up from breakfast and did the dishes and made Mom's bed.

I cooked meat for tacos and grated the cheese and cut up some old tomatoes and set the table.

Then I went outside and waited.

Berk and Sadie and Jane were making up a dance in the street. They'd all crunch down and then Berk would count 1 2 3 and they'd jump up, with their arms in the air and yell, "HOORAY!"

I laughed.

"That's what we're going to do at the beginning of the dance for the opening part," Berk said.

"I thought you were doing tightrope," I said.

"I'm doing tons of things."

"I'm doing three acts," said Sadie.

"I think I'm just doing this," said Jane.

I nodded. "It looks very professional."

They practiced so long the sun started to go down and Sadie and Jane's mom came to pick them up.

And then it was just Berkeley.

She came and sat by me on the steps. "Where's Mom?"

"I don't know," I said.

She nodded. "I told Grant that he should be in the circus."

I looked over at his trailer. "When was he out?"

"Earlier," she said. "You were inside. He was jogging and he was really really sweaty."

This was the second time Grant exercised. Bart would want to know.

"He asked what we were doing and I told him about the circus and he said he might do an act."

I sighed. Berk was telling everyone. Like it was real. Like it was going to happen.

"What can he do?" I asked.

She shrugged. "He said maybe belly dancing."

I giggled. I couldn't help it.

She said, "What? He said he was really good."

I giggled harder.

"What?"

"I think he would be good," I said, still giggling.

"What's so funny?" she asked.

"Do you know what belly dancing is?"

"No."

I didn't really know either but I went out on the road and tied my shirt up to show my stomach. Then as the day turned to night, I belly danced, circling around like I was some exotic lady from Bali or Egypt.

Berk squealed and came and belly danced with me, both of us laughing and laughing and laughing and for the first time, in a long time, I thought maybe, somehow, things would be okay.

That night Berk and I watched the Shanghai Circus and they maybe were the best in the entire world.

We ate tacos.

We cleaned up.

We brushed our teeth.

I combed her hair.

I entered a contest for a family vacation to Orlando and one for a two-hundred-dollar Amex card which were both new contests.

Then we went to bed.

At eleven p.m. I heard Mom's car pull up.

I watched her get out thinking maybe she'd be in her shiny new blouse and sexy jeans and lipstick with Tandi but really she was wearing a gray work shirt, which meant she'd taken a night shift at an office building.

She had bags of groceries and she looked tired.

But this meant, I hoped, that she had enough money now to pay for day care.

Things really were going to be okay.

CHAPTER 56

Morning.

Mom yelling, "Girls, it's almost time to go."

I sat up, my head pounding.

Berkeley climbed out of bed, her hair messy and her eyes hollow. She hadn't slept so well, you could tell. She stood by my bed and whispered, "Am I going with you again?"

"I don't know," I said.

Mom came in. "What in the world? You two get dressed. We're leaving in five minutes!"

Berkeley's eyes fell.

"It's going to be okay," I whispered. Maybe she found a day care. I'm sure she'd found a day care. "I promise."

She nodded.

We got dressed.

We held hands.

We went to the front room.

At the table she pulled out bowls. Cheerios. Some bananas. She'd bought bananas. She was humming.

"How was yesterday," Mom asked.

I looked at Berk. She looked at me. "It was okay," I said.

"Good!" Mom said. Her voice was cheery and different. "Thank you so much, Sissy," she said to me.

A pit grew in my stomach.

We ate.

Mom started singing and then she said, "Oh! I almost forgot!"

She opened the fridge. "I got you girls something." She pulled out two trays. "Lunchables! With Capri Suns!"

I swallowed. Those things were expensive. We never got them. I wondered if the price of one Lunchable would pay for a day of day care.

So I took Berk to school another day. Tuesday.

And I didn't talk to anyone the whole day. I tried to be invisible.

We didn't get caught but we got close a few times. Like when a gym teacher or maybe just a man wearing short shorts and a whistle around his neck, when he saw me come out of the supply closet and he said, "What were you doing in there?"

At first I said nothing because I was having a heart attack. But then I said, "I got lost."

And he said, "You got lost?"

And then I said, "I had a contagious illness so I didn't

get to come to school for a few months and now that I'm back I get confused."

He stared at me.

"What kind of illness?"

And I said, "It's private."

And he said, "It's private?"

And I said, "It's illegal to tell you because of my healthcare rights."

And he said,

And I said,

And he said,

And I said,

And he said, "Get to class."

And I said, "Okay."

Also, I didn't meet Bart for lunch but I did eat Lunchables in the closet and talk about the Shanghai Circus.

I took her to school Wednesday. Mom made us do Wednesday.

My stomach was in knots the whole fat day. I said fifty-six prayers that no one would find her and we made it.

Mom worked late again.

Me and Berk watched the the Big Apple Circus and I made us frozen pizza.

Before bed I did twenty-two contests, including a chance to win a hundred boxes of Totino's frozen pizzas even though I had no idea where we'd put them if we won.

I took her to school Thursday. This time I tried to be more prepared.

I made Berkeley keep the light out in the closet but I brought her a headlamp we found at the KOA once and also I had a few old candy bars from Halloween and I told her that if she could not go to the bathroom the whole day, she could have them and she did it!

I looked for Bart in the halls but not really.

I didn't see him.

At home, we watched Circus Oz of Australia and we ate macaroni and cheese with peas in it for energy.

Delilah came by and said, "Where's your mom?"

And I said, "I don't know."

And she said, "School still going okay?"

And I said, "Fine."

She looked at Berk who was munching on a doughnut Delilah'd brought us. "How's the new day care."

She stopped munching. Looked at me. Please. Please. Please.

"Fine," she said. Picked up another doughnut. I let out a breath I didn't know I'd been holding.

"Well, I miss you ladies. Melody was saying she missed you all, too. Why don't you come over after school tomorrow and watch some shows?"

They were talking about us? She and Melody. I wondered if other people in the neighborhood were, too. I wondered if that was good or bad. Should I tell her? Should I tell Melody? Would they help us or would they think bad of Mom?

I said, "Maybe we can come watch later," and Berk said, "Do you want to be in our circus?"

I said, "Berk. Delilah doesn't want to be in the circus."

But Delilah, she said, "Sure I do." Just like that. Without asking what it was or what that meant or where it would be or what the heck Berk was talking about.

Sure.

And then she had to go because *The Real Housewives of Orange County* was on.

Mom was late again.

I took Berk to school Friday.

Headlamp. Soft Batch cookies instead of candy and I had us both wear all black.

This time I did see Bart but not on purpose.

I was passing the gym on my way up to the closet after English and the door was propped open.

I looked in and Bart was standing against wall. A gym

teacher, the same one I'd seen, with the shorts and the whistle was talking to him. Loud. He was saying, "You can't keep doing this and expect to pass."

Bart nodded. The man's voice was so, so mean.

"You know you're on thin ice."

Bart started fiddling with his watch.

"Hey," the guy said. Bart kept fiddling. "HEY!"

Bart looked at him. My hands started to sweat just watching him. How big the guy was and how little Bart looked. He'd never seemed little to me before.

"Look at me when I'm talking. Look. At. Me. You come to class. You get here on time. You get changed. You participate. I don't care about what your mom or anyone else says. You're twelve. Act like it."

Bart nodded. Mumbled something. Then he did this, Bart turned, he turned and looked right at me and as he did it, so did the coach.

I froze.

"Can I help you?" the man said.

I . . .

I . . .

"Can. I. Help. You." His voice echoed through the gym and out the door and into my bones.

So then I ran.

I ran.

I ran.

And when I got to the supply closet I burst in, my lungs burning and my heart pounding and Berk said, "What's wrong? Are we caught?"

That afternoon on the walk home I tried to decide if I should find Bart. Maybe he needed me as much as I needed him even though I didn't really need him but maybe I did.

I also tried to figure out if that coach recognized me and now I had to be extra careful in the halls and how I'd messed up. I shouldn't have stayed there to listen. I should have gone fast. Quiet. Gotten out of there. Straight to Berk.

Take care of your sister.

Take care of your sister.

Take care of your sister.

I felt sick to my stomach.

Sick for Berk.

Sick for me.

Sick for Bart who got yelled at by a dumb-bum coach.

Sick for Mom because she was doing this. Why was she doing this?

Sick for Dad because he didn't know how bad things were.

When we got home, Berk played with her friends and I lay on the couch, my belly aching.

Carlene knocked on the door. I saw her and I didn't move.

"Is Olivia home?" she asked Berk.

I don't know what Berk said but Carlene went away and I was glad even though it was Carlene and maybe she was going to help me or give me details on Monster Jam.

I wanted everyone to go away.

"What's for dinner?" Berk asked when she finally came in from playing.

I pointed at the cereal on the table.

After she ate, my stomach got worse and my head started to hurt too and, "Can we watch a circus?" she asked.

"Yeah. We can." I turned it on.

Cirque Mana of France.

Trapeze.

My head pounding.

My stomach aching.

Trapeze.

Swinging.

And swinging.

Swinging.

And Berk.

Berk lay on her Barbie blanket with her dolls all around her. She always watched TV like this.

I watched Berk watch. The freckles on her cheeks. Her lips and her perfect little nose. Her mouth opening and closing in anticipation of every move, every jump, every catch. Clapping after each act.

Before I knew it, I was clapping, too. The pain starting to go away a little.

Then, right in the middle of the lions, Mom got home. Banged through the door.

"Hey," she said.

"Hey," I said.

She looked tired again. And in the office cleaning work shirt.

"Why are you working late?" I asked.

She shrugged, put her keys on the table. "I'm saving for something."

My stomach clenched again. She was saving for something?

She walked over. Sat on the floor with Berk. Pulled her onto her lap.

After a few minutes she said, "Why are we watching this?" Mom said.

"Because we're having a neighborhood circus and we have to get ideas," Berk said.

Mom looked at me. "A neighborhood circus? Who is?"

Now Berk looked at me but I didn't look at either of them. I closed my eyes instead. The headache was back.

"We are. They asked us to do a circus at the HOA meeting. Tell her, Liv," Berk said.

I rubbed my forehead.

"They asked you to do what? What are you talking about?"

I stood up.

"Olivia."

I felt dizzy.

"Olivia!"

I walked down the hall.

"Olivia! Get back here."

I closed my bedroom door.

I put all the blankets and clothes and stuffed animals and bags and everything I could find on the bed and then I crawled under it.

CHAPTER 57

As a reward for Berkeley sitting in the broom closet at my school, Mom dropped us off before work at the rec center on Saturday just like she said she would.

I thought about asking her if it was okay to swim even with a contagious illness but then I didn't. I didn't ask her anything about the illness or what she said to the counselor at school or how she had started lying or what she was saving for instead of taking care of us.

Instead I ate Lunchables and went to the rec center.

Berkeley loved going to the pool—especially the indoor pool where they had a pirate ship and water-slides and spray guns. She was a fish and she always made friends and most of all she loved the waterslide, which she could only do if I went with her which I didn't love but I did it anyway.

Except today.

Today I wanted to do nothing.

I wanted to float in the lazy river and be no one.

Berkeley said, "Should we go down the slide? Do you want to go down the slide?"

And I said, "No."

"Why not?" We were in the ladies' locker room and she had been bouncing up and down and singing "Jingle Bells" and whispering to herself, which she did a lot, but when I said no she stopped.

I was stuffing our things in an empty locker and it would probably get stolen anyway because I didn't get a lock and she said, "No?"

"No. I don't really feel like the slide today. Let's just do the lazy river."

I tried to slam the locker closed but it wouldn't go, so then I had to take everything out and put it back in and some naked lady next to me said, "Honey child, that thing is not going to fit," and instead of saying, "Yes it will. Mind your own business," I said, "It won't?"

And she said, "No way in this universe."

And I said, "Thank you," and then she went to the shower and this all put me in a way worse mood, so much that I had almost forgot that my sad little sister who I had just crushed was standing there.

I looked at her. Her lip was quivering and I could tell that this was not the day to say no to Berkeley. A five-year-old can only put up with so much.

I took a deep breath, made a decision in the gut place, and said, "I'm sorry, Berk. We can go on the slide as many times as you want."

I could do the lazy river when she felt like playing on the pirate ship.

"YAY!!! Yayayayayayayayayayayayayayaay!" she yelled.

Everyone looked at us but I didn't care. It really was the best moment of the whole entire week and I told my gut thank you.

CHAPTER 58

Before I knew it, we were standing on the stairs for the waterslide. The lines were long on Saturday. I'd looked around and my favorite lifeguard, Troy, who had almost saved my life, was not there.

Instead it was the lady who blew her whistle at Berkeley for hanging on the rope one time, which she was just barely barely not even really touching.

Berkeley was chatting with two other kids in front of us and I stared at the lazy river, which had tons of people.

I saw a dad running in the river with two kids hanging off him, laughing their faces off and there was a lady sitting on the side and she was laughing, too, and I didn't know for sure but that was the mom and they were going to go get ice cream after and maybe even fancy hamburgers and then they'd all go home and watch *America's Funniest Home Videos* together or something.

I felt tears start to come so I stopped staring at the dumb-bum lazy river.

Across the way, through a glass wall, was the competition pool where people who really knew how to swim did laps and where the swim team went for practice and swim meets.

I wished I was good at swimming and that I could go and do laps back and forth and back and forth and back and forth and forget about everything.

Right now, the play pools and waterslides were packed. But the competition pool was quiet. It looked like a whole other world over there.

One where not everyone got to go.

Only certain people.

A group was forming on the side of the pool.

It was a water aerobics class.

There were a bunch of ladies. Big ladies. Old ladies. Mom ladies. One even looked like Mrs. Sydney Gunnerson. Was that Mrs. Sydney Gunnerson?

I squinted to see better but it didn't help. It looked a lot like her. She wasn't the type of person I would think would do water aerobics. The clock said it was almost twelve so she would be way done selling dolls by now.

Then, just as the waterslide line started to move, I saw something I was not expecting.

I saw something that almost made me gasp out loud.

~

I saw a boy.

Getting into the water and starting to do water aerobics with all the old people.

I saw someone I thought I was starting to love and who I watched get in trouble.

I saw Bart.

CHAPTER 59

When I saw Bart waving his arms in the water, I knew he was really just trying to make me laugh. And I did laugh. "You're doing water aerobics," I yelled.

He said, "Yes. Is it funny?"

And I said, "Yes."

Then he jumped out of the pool and I dropped Berkeley's hand and even though there was glass between us, and a hundred kids screaming and moms yelling and the lifeguards blowing their whistle and someone hitting an echo-y ball against the wall, why were they doing that? Even through all that, I heard his voice and he said, "I've been trying to find you."

And I said, "I'm so sorry! I'm also sorry you got in trouble."

And then I ran up the stairs to the opening at the slide and even though there were all these people ahead of me, they said, "GO! GO! GO to him!" And even though a part of me thought, this is so wrong, another part of me thought, this is so right.

I jumped on the slide headfirst and went through

the tube faster than anyone had ever gone before and when the slide went outside the building to the part where you can see the parking lot—this is actually a pretty cool thing about the slide, by the way—at that part, there were thousands of people in the parking lot holding signs that said, LOVE with all your HEART!

"I will!" I yelled as I zoomed to the end of the water-slide and he was there waiting for me and he was wearing his tank top and puffy jeans but I didn't care.

When he saw me, his whole face lit up and he said, "I love you," and I said, "I love you," and I ran to him and he picked me up over his head and I put my arms in the air like I was in the Olympics and the whole place was screaming and yelling and cheering.

The boy said, "Go."

And I said, "What?"

And he said, "Go."

He pointed to the slide.

We were at the top. Berkeley, I guess, had already gone down.

I sat down. "GO!" someone yelled.

The water was rushing and my stomach was rumbling and I wondered if I really did love Bart.

Then someone pushed me and I went down the waterslide.

~

When I got out and I was soaked and hyperventilating because I do not like the waterslide, I looked through the glass to see if he was still there.

A blond lady in a swimsuit and pants that said ZUMBA on the butt was jumping around on the deck and all the old people and ladies were in the pool mimicking her.

In the corner, in the back, was Bart.

My Bart.

Really there.

Doing Aqua Zumba.

....

Dear Dad,

How did you know when you were in love? I'm asking for a friend who likes this boy and thinks it may be love but she doesn't know anything about him except that he's nice. And he's smart. And he works in a kitchen. And he takes a water aerobics class. Is that strange? Would you ever take a water aerobics class? I don't think you would. Should the girl not like him?

Also, we're so happy! Mom seems better than ever and so am I and so is Berkeley. Carlene hasn't said anything about Las Vegas but she did say that if you wanted to come you could just call her dad. I told her you probably would when you got back to the ranger station. Can you do that? Do you still have his number? I can get it for you.

Also, I think Mrs. Sydney Gunnerson goes to water aerobics, too. She may know the boy my friend likes because after class the teacher, the boy, and Mrs. Sydney Gunnerson were talking. I only know this because my friend told me and my friend knows Mrs. Sydney

Gunnerson because my friend comes over here all the time because that's what friends do. They hang out together. Or they live by each other.

Me and Berk really are putting on a circus. Plans are moving ahead and we are getting an elephant and a lion and a boy who can eat fire.

If you can come to Las Vegas or not come, it's fine but I would love it if you could tell me. Or if you want to come to the circus, I think we're doing it right after school gets out.

Love your
daughter,
Olivia

P.S. Did you know there is a National Park Tour Giveaway? I've entered it a few times. Maybe it will have Bryce!

....

CHAPTER 60

On Monday, I wanted to find Bart.

So much.

I wanted to talk to him about the pool because I hadn't dared after I got off the slide and then I had to follow Berkeley around the pirate ship and by the time I went to look in there again, he was gone.

At school I didn't have a chance to go to the cafeteria because I had to eat with Berkeley and I didn't want to take the risk to go to the gym when I knew he'd be there and also Monday was a bad day because in between two class breaks there were people by the closet door so I couldn't slip in, which meant I left Berk alone for hours. And even though she said she was okay when I finally went, she was shaking and I could tell she'd been crying.

Crying.

We couldn't do this much longer.

Now I was home from school and Mom was home early for the first time in weeks and inside taking a nap.

And Berk was inside, too, watching cartoons with Sadie and Jane.

And I was outside on the tramp, hoping for Bart.

Hoping and hoping and saying, Please come, please come, please come, please come, please come, please come, please come, please come.

And then,

Like magic.

I opened my eyes and there he was.

He was in a different tank top this time but the same pants and he seemed happy and he was cute. I'm sorry but he was.

I tried to stop it but my whole body tingled.

He climbed onto the tramp and bounced a little.

"What's been going on?"

I smiled.

"Nothing."

He started jumping.

He said, "Can you do this?"

He did a front flip, which hello, of course I could.

I stood up and he got to the side and I did one. Then two. Then three in a row.

"Whoa. Show-off."

"You started it," I said.

So then he did a front handspring, which was easy.

Then I did a backflip and he said, "I can't do those."

"You can't?"

He shrugged. "I mean I could but I don't feel like it because I think they're dumb."

I said, "You're dumb," and he said, "You're dumb," and then he laughed and then laughed and then there was definitely something different between us.

I sat down and he sat down.

I smiled, "I saw you on Saturday."

"Where?"

"Somewhere."

"Where?"

"At the rec center."

His face flushed. "No, you didn't."

"Yes I did."

"No, you didn't."

"I did."

We were sitting facing each other, our knees almost touching, and at first I thought it would be funny to tell him but then I saw it was not funny. He was starting to sweat. It felt like the lunchroom situation all over again.

"It's okay," I said.

He shook his head. "I wasn't there. You didn't see me."

"I did," I said. My voice was quiet. "It's okay. You can tell me stuff."

He looked at his hands.

He stood up. "I have to go."

"You have to go?"

He was about to get off the tramp and I was trying to

say don't go. Please don't go. Please. I've been waiting for you. Please.

But before I could get that all out, Grant's truck came barreling down the street.

We both turned to see it, and Bart jumped down flat on the tramp. "Get down get down get down," he whispered loud.

I got down. At least this time it was on the tramp not the hard old ground.

Grant pulled up in front of his trailer, his heavy metal music blasting so loud the trees were shaking. He turned it off and said a bunch of words so bad some of them I didn't even understand.

He got out of the truck and slammed the door. Then opened it and slammed it again. And again and again.

I had never seen him this mad. In fact, I don't think I'd seen *anyone* so mad, even Dad, and it was scary.

"Wow," I whispered.

"Shhh," Bart said, and he grabbed my hand. It would have been nice and I would have maybe felt embarrassed but things were too tense. Plus, he was trembling.

"Are you okay?" I whispered.

He shook his head, still watching Grant who was now kicking things. He was kicking an old gas can, he kicked a pile of boxes. He walked over to Melody's house and kicked the side of her trailer.

She came out and he said, "Stay away from me."

And she said, "What's going on Grant? Where's Bob?"

She spoke calm and collected. Like she was trying to soothe him. I realized maybe Melody cared about Grant even though he was such a dumb-bum.

"I don't care where Bob is and you stay away from me."

He climbed up on his trailer then.

"What is he doing," Bart whispered.

I had no idea. I had really no idea and I told Bart that.

Grant started swearing again and kicking more things off the top of the roof, which were leaves and dirty water and then an old bucket which was ours, and how did that get up there?

Melody stood below watching with her hands on her hips.

Then Mrs. Sydney Gunnerson came out. I looked at Bart to see if he was thinking, "Oh, I know that lady. I do Water Zumba with her." But his face didn't flinch or say anything.

"What's going on?" Mrs. Sydney Gunnerson asked Melody.

"No idea. I think we should call Bob."

"We should call the cops," Mrs. Sydney Gunnerson said.

Melody looked at her. "No. He's just upset."

He was ignoring all of this. Instead he was climbing back down and then getting his dumb radio and then climbing back up.

"Grant," Melody said. "What are you doing?"

He ignored her. He got up there and then he turned on a song and started singing with it like he was in a concert in an amphitheater or something. "Welcome to the jungle," he screamed.

Now Tandi came out.

And Carlene.

"Grant!" Melody said.

He kept screaming.

Randy was standing by his trailer watering his pots and watching.

Baby George and his mom.

When Grant got to the end of the song, he chucked his radio onto the ground.

And we all sort of gasped as it shattered to pieces on the concrete.

"I DON'T CARE!" he yelled.

My body got cold then. This wasn't a joke at all.

Bart squeezed my hand and Grant really did look so bad.

He was crying and he'd climbed back down and was kicking things.

He was kicking the grass. He kicked his own truck.

And then he acted like he was going to kick Mrs. Sydney Gunnerson's Cadillac and she said, "Oh no you don't, you old coward."

"What did you call me?" he yelled. "What did you just call me?"

I thought Mrs. Sydney Gunnerson would be scared because he was scary; he was out of control. But Mrs. Sydney Gunnerson didn't look shaken at all. She just stood there and said, "You leave my Caddy alone, you brute. Just because you don't know how to live your life don't mean you can ruin ours."

This got him hopping. Hopping up and down.

"Oh you think I'm ruining your life, Sydney? Who ruined whose life? Huh? Who ruined whose life?"

Mrs. Sydney Gunnerson said, "Grant, I am not getting involved in whatever you're talking about but if you don't get off my property I will call the police and they will not waste a second hauling your sorry butt into jail."

Grant was going crazy now. He was squatting and pointing to himself. Stabbing himself really hard with his pointer finger. "You're going to call the cops on me? ME?" He looked around wildly. "What have I ever done to anyone? What? Has every woman gone crazy?"

He was making no sense. I was going to tell this to Bart but he was still gripping my hand hard and he hadn't moved an inch.

So I decided to hold still. Wait.

"Calm down, Grant," Paul the MMA fighter said. He was walking up and Grant said, "You want to beat me up, Paul? You wanna?"

And Mrs. Sydney Gunnerson said, "Do it."

And Melody said, "Someone stop this. Will someone please stop this? Please?"

No one made a move except Paul, who I was pretty sure could kill Grant if he wanted.

Melody came down her stairs. "Please. Someone. Stop this."

Grant pointed at her. "Go inside."

That's when Mom came out.

I was shocked because for a while now she hardly ever came out unless it was to get in her car and drive away. And especially not to get involved in neighborhood fights. But now she was out of the house and the entire air changed.

Everyone looked at her.

She stood big even though she wasn't big. She stood big and said, "Grant. Is this about that woman?"

His eyes were wild. What woman? What was she talking about? Trinity? That was like two years ago.

"What do you know, LeAnn?" he said.

Mom didn't move. She had him in a death stare.

"Did she hurt you?" Mom asked.

Grant's face started to tremble.

He shook his head. "You don't know what you're talking about."

"Come over here," Mom said.

"I'm kind of busy," Grant said.

"I can see that and I don't care. I need to tell you something and then you can let Paul over there beat the crap out of you."

Grant looked at Paul. Then back at Mom. He was sweating and huffing and you could tell things were turning in his head.

"Come on, Grant," she said. "I need to go back to my nap."

"He's out of control, LeAnn. Let me take care of this," Paul said.

Mom scoffed. "I'm not scared of old Grant. He would never hurt me, right, Grant?"

Grant swore, then he said, "Nah."

And Mom said, "Back off, Paul."

Paul took a step back.

Then Grant, he walked over to our porch and my mom, in her ratty old muumuu and her hair up in her sleeping bun, she leaned down and whispered something in his ear.

We all watched.

This time the whole place froze.

For my mom.

What could she possibly be saying?

Grant listened.

He nodded.

She kept talking.

And I swear this really happened, a tear rolled down his cheek.

And then, like she did stuff like this every day, she did this: She came down the steps and she hugged him.

Sweaty old dumb-bum Grant.

Hard.

My mom hugged Grant hard.

I bit my lip. Didn't look at Bart, who didn't look at me, either, I was sure. The whole thing was too much.

And Grant started really crying then. Heaving and sobbing, and Mom, holding him.

Holding him and saying, "I know. I know. I know. It's okay. I know."

And him nodding and wiping his nose and nodding.

The whole world on pause for the two of them.

Then, as fast as it had started, it was over.

He pulled away, wiped his nose with the back of his hand, took a deep dark breath and said, "I'm going inside."

And then he did.

CHAPTER 61

"What did she say?" Bart wanted to know. We were still on the tramp.

I shrugged.

The whole place was silent, wind chimes tinkling in the afternoon breeze.

No one ever would have known that just a few moments ago somebody was about to get his brains busted in by his neighbor.

"Are they friends?" Bart asked.

Were they? And the more I thought about it, yes. They were friends.

I said, "Yes."

"They are?" he asked again.

"Sure," I said.

This seemed important to Bart. Then he said, "Can you ask her what she said?"

Bart was looking at me. "Can you?"

I nodded. "I'll try later."

"Why not now?" he said. He wasn't holding my hand anymore and anything that had felt different only ten minutes before had vanished.

"I don't know," I said. "She's probably sleeping."

"She just went inside."

"I know but she goes to sleep really fast."

The two of us lay there. Me thinking about how strange this whole afternoon had turned out. Him, I have no idea what he was thinking but probably about my mom.

"I wish my mom was like your mom," he said.

"What?"

"You know," he said. "She seemed tough."

I couldn't believe that was what he thought.

"She's not tough," I said, trying to keep my voice steady.

He was quiet.

I was quiet.

Then he said, "I know you bring Berkeley to school."

I looked at him, my stomach a washing machine. "How do you know that?"

"It's not like she's invisible."

Oh crap oh crap oh crap. If Bart had seen her, who else had?

For some reason, and I know this is stupid, for some reason, I kind of thought she *was* invisible. I thought we both were because no one had noticed us by now.

"When did you find out?"

"I saw you guys back a week ago when you were supposed to meet me but then you didn't."

"You saw us?"

He nodded. Then he said, "And I've seen you guys every day after."

Now my gut ached.

"Why didn't you come help me?" I said, my heart pounding. "Why didn't you say something? Why didn't you talk to me?"

Everything started coming out and I should have stopped myself but I didn't. "I don't have anyone to help me. Why didn't you say something? Where were you? Where did you see us?" and on and on and on and on and on.

When I finally stopped I felt hot and red and he looked hot and red and he said . . .

He said . . .

"Sorry."

Sorry.

I said nothing, my eyes tired.

He said, "I'm really sorry. I thought you didn't want my help because you didn't meet me."

He said, "I should have said something. I should've done something. I'm not good at doing things."

He kept talking. "I don't like school and you saw.

You saw. I don't belong there. The teachers hate me."

I said nothing.

"Every day, every day," he said, "I try to make myself stay. Try to stay. Go to class. Sit still. Sit there. Sit there. Listen. Do what they say. Focus. They say focus, focus, Harrison," he hesitated, his voice wobbly. Then he said, "If I miss any more school I might get held back so I have to go but I'm trying not to get noticed. I want no one to see me."

He looked at me. "It's better for me if no one sees me. Like you and Berkeley."

I nodded.

He nodded.

And we sat there.

And sat there.

And sat there.

Finally, he said, "You know, because of the FBI."

CHAPTER 62

The sun was easing behind the lake, the colors splattered across the sky. Oranges. Purples. Pinks. And even though I was mad and confused and sad and mad mad mad, even though that, it felt good to be outside, with him.

He tapped my hand with his finger. I looked at him. "I've been watching out for you guys though. I made sure you were safe."

I took a breath.

And even if I didn't know how he could be watching out for us, even if there was no way he could be keeping us safe, even though it didn't make any sense, I took a real breath for the first time in a long long time.

....

Dear Dad,

   I guess Grant has a really bad temper. There was almost a fight but Mom broke it up. I'd never seen her do something like that before. Sometimes I think I don't know her so well. But you know her really well, right? Is she tough? Did she used to be tough?

Also, do you still love her? I guess you don't. Why don't you? Did she change? Or is she the same? Did you change? How did you decide to stop loving her? Is it something you can turn off and turn on?

When Grant got mad and Mom stopped the fight, I asked her what happened, what she'd said, and she told me that Grant is in love. I said how do you know? And she said, did you see how mad he got?

I've been thinking about that. Does love make you mad? Why? And if it does, why does it? Mom does seem mad a lot and I realized maybe it's because she still loves you. Is that why? Do you know? And if she does but you aren't here, that means it doesn't end even if the person you love is done loving you. I think that sucks.

Are you done loving her?

Also, Mom really hates our neighbor Melody and I don't understand why. Melody's husband is gone all the time and sometimes he comes back and she's happy but most of the time he's gone and Melody is all alone. Mom's not alone. She has me and Berk and does she still have you? Do you guys call each other?

Do you text each other? Do you send her letters and tell her you miss her? Or do you not miss her at all? Even if you don't love her anymore, wouldn't you still miss her? Because you lived together and got married and had kids together so I think that would mean you would miss her, that you'd be friends, or at least think about each other but maybe not?

Does anyone love someone forever? And what happens to all those good things and memories when you stop? Do they disappear? Have you forgotten when you used to dance with her in the living room or when we all sat on that dock by the lake one time and you said, this is what I love. Were you lying?

Do you lie?

Do you have a girlfriend?

Olivia

....

I stared at the screen.

I shouldn't send it. I knew that.

But he probably never read them anyway.

The night was dark and out the window I saw Grant sitting on his front step. Bob was talking to him and he was nodding. Then Bob went inside and Grant, he looked up at the moon, and I could see he'd been crying. He wiped his nose with his shirt.

I stared at him.

Then I clicked *send*.

CHAPTER 63

The next day when I took Berk to school, I was more careful.

I made sure to take extra precautions like varying our routine and taking different routes. I even drew a map of the school and potential exits in case we were compromised:

I didn't see Bart but I knew he was watching and I hoped he was helping. Not waiting to turn us in.

My goals at school were these:
Take care of Berkeley.
Smile.
Keep everything normal.
Draw no attention to myself.
Not get caught.

My goals at home were these:
Make Mom eat.
Figure out why Mom is working late and not putting Berk in day care.
Make Mom talk more. (She had gotten back to being

quieter except to tell Berk she wouldn't sing at the circus.)

Do the laundry.

Change the air filters on the swamp cooler.

Clean the bathroom, especially the floor.

Enter more contests.

I made all my school goals on Monday but the home goals were harder.

I changed the filters.

I did the laundry.

I sort of cleaned the bathroom but it was gross.

I entered more contests, even ones that weren't so good like I could win a complete set of Louis L'Amour books, which I don't even know who that is.

I did all that but the Mom goals were harder.

She got home late again and didn't talk even though I waited up and when I got her cereal and Diet Coke in the morning, she only took the Coke.

Same thing on Tuesday.

Then, on Wednesday night, she got in a huge huge screaming fight with Tandi on our front patio.

Tandi was yelling at her about work. Something about not doing a good job on a house. One she was covering for Tandi.

And Mom said something quiet.

She had been watching *Wheel of Fortune* and me and Berk were playing Operation but without batteries because they ran out, when Tandi came over and told her to come talk to her outside.

At first the conversation was quiet. But then it got loud.

Tandi yelled again. "I got you this job and I'm not going to lose it because of you."

Mom: "I'm sorry, Tandi, okay? I've had a lot going on."

Tandi: "Oh come on, LeAnn. You've had a year to get your crap together."

Then Tandi went on and on about things that had been happening. Houses. Clients. Money. She said something about me and Berk. I held my breath.

Did she know?

Did she know?

But then she didn't say anything about school or day care so maybe she didn't. And was Mom going to lose her job?

I looked at Berk and she looked at me. Both of us frozen. I took her hand.

Finally, when it all ended and Tandi said, "You need to get it together, LeAnn. And soon."

Mom said: "Get off my property."

And then Tandi laughed like this was the most hilarious thing in the whole world.

Mom came inside.

I waited. Maybe she'd come sit down and tell us everything.

But she walked back to her room and slammed the door.

And Berk took the guy's liver out.

CHAPTER 64

That night I made a decision.

What if Mom really did lose her job? What if things were falling apart? What if Mom couldn't get it together, what then? Would we lose the house? Would we have to live on the streets?

I had to do something. I was trying to help her, trying and trying and trying but it wasn't working.

So I decided.

I had to find Dad.

Right?

Right?

I listened for my gut and it said nothing.

I went to the computer.

Bryce National Park.

Greyhound buses?

Taxi rides?

Craigslist carpool board?

I could go. I could go there this weekend. I could find him.

I printed up the map of Bryce.

I wrote up a list of things I should take.

I didn't know the best way to get there, though.
So then I did this:

....

Dear Bart,

I'm going to try to get to Bryce to get my
dad to help us. Can you help me? Do you
think going on a Greyhound bus is good or
should I do one of those Uber ride things? The
Greyhound will take twice the time but I don't
know about the ride stuff. What do you think?
And you could come but you don't have to but
you could. Will you email me back and if you
can't, it's okay. I'll find you at school.

From,
Olivia,
Your friend

....

Please God. Please let Bart come.
That he'll do this with me.
I'm coming Dad.

CHAPTER 65

I didn't sleep.

When the sun came up, I got up.

Got dressed.

Put my hair in a ponytail.

Stared at myself in the mirror.

Walked into the kitchen.

Checked the computer.

Didn't get an email from Bart but I'd find him and he'd come with me probably. I thought maybe he'd come. Because he loves to travel.

Please.

Please let him come with me.

Entered eight more contests, including a coastal Dream Home Giveaway in Merritt Island, Florida.

Sat down.

Ate Honey Bunches of Oats.

Said hi to Berkeley.

Got her Honey Bunches of Oats.

Mom came out.

She had on lipstick.

She looked at me.

She said, "You look strange."

I looked at her.

I said, "No I don't."

She said, "Yes you do. Did you sleep very well?"

I wanted to say, "No, I didn't because are you going to lose your job and why are you working at another job at night, and if you are, why aren't you putting Berk in day care and what are you saving for and why won't you talk to me and what is going on? I am going to find Dad and if I go alone I might get lost and wind up in the wilderness and then no one will know where I am and three years later they'll dig me up and I'll just be a very small bone."

I wanted to say all that.

But instead I said, "I'm fine."

And she sighed.

Then she drove me and Berk to school. It was a dark day, the whole world damp and cold.

Berkeley said, "Something bad's going to happen."

I glanced back at her, my heart thumping. Was this her gut telling me not to go?

She had her hand on the window.

I looked at Mom whose face was tight.

"Why do you say that Berkeley?" Mom asked.

She shrugged. "I can feel it. It's like when Peep's sand castle got washed out."

Peep and the Big Wide World was Berk's favorite cartoon.

Mom gripped the steering wheel. "It's a perfectly wonderful day," she said. "We need the rain. It makes me feel refreshed."

Her voice was hollow. We were in a play.

Once Mom dropped us off, I stood in the crowd and searched for Bart.

Searched and searched.

"What are you doing?" Berk asked.

"Just a second."

"Don't we need to hurry?"

I nodded. We did. We did need to hurry and where was he?

Then someone said something. They said, "Olivia." I turned, shoved Berkeley behind me, and turned. It was Carlene.

And Bonnie.

"Why's Berk here?" Carlene said.

My throat closed. Carlene looked concerned. Bonnie looked not concerned. At all.

"I'm taking her across the street," I said, and pointed at a house. "To a day care."

"There's a day care over there?" Bonnie said. "It looks like a drug house."

"It's not a drug house," I said, even though it did look like a drug house.

Carlene said to Bonnie, "I'll meet you inside," and Bonnie said, "No. I'll wait."

"Really," Carlene said. "You'll be late."

Bonnie gave me a glare. Then she said fine and went inside.

Carlene turned to me. "I can walk her over with you."

"Oh, that's okay. I can do it. You should get to class."

She nodded. Then she said to Berk, "Do you like it there?"

Berk didn't say anything and my heart was breaking.

"It's just temporary. We're trying to find a different place," I said, squeezing Berk's hand.

Carlene said, "I know. I'm so sorry about what happened with Tandi yesterday. I don't know what her problem is."

"It's okay," I said.

"It's not okay. She can be such a witch. I love your mom. She's so cool."

I almost laughed.

I almost cried, too.

And mostly I tried not to throw my arms around Carlene and tell her everything and tell her I missed her and that I wished things were how they used to be and how I wanted to go to the Monster Jam and that I was so grateful she told dumb-bum Bonnie to shut up and that I was going to try to find my dad because everything was falling apart and I was going to ask Bart if he could go with me but maybe she could go with me and would she dare go with me? We used to play in the river and do scary things like trap a beaver that could have had rabies.

I tried not to do those things. In fact, I didn't. I just said, "My mom is cool, I guess."

She smiled. Then she said, "Well, I'll see you later."

And I said, "Yeah, I'll see you later."

And then she turned and went into the school.

Berkeley said, "I like Carlene."

And I said, "I like her, too."

By then most everyone was inside. The first bell had rung.

I walked Berkeley down the sidewalk to the side of the building.

"We've never gone this way," she said.

"I know," I said. "I just wanted to try something different."

"Why?"

"Because it's safer."

"Safer? Safer from what?"

I said, "It's safer in case there's a fire."

This was stupid and I think Berk knew it was stupid but she just held my hand as we walked through the gym where I'd seen Bart and where maybe I'd see him again? Maybe the gym coach made him mop the floors or wipe the walls before school every day? But there was no one there, so we walked through the gym and then waited by the door until the second bell rang.

"When I say go, we're going to run." We were clear on the other side of the building from the closet.

"Okay," she said, without asking questions.

Soon the halls were empty.

In some ways, this was not smart. You can blend in when there're hundreds of people.

But on the other hand, if you do it that way, there're hundreds of people to see you.

So we waited.

Once there was no one in sight, I said, "Now!"

Then she and I, holding hands, ran through the hall, me trying to keep my steps as quiet as I could, her stomping her boots like she was in the army but I couldn't do anything about that.

Luckily, as we were going up the stairs the national anthem came on and we made it to the closet before it was over, avoiding any teachers or people coming late or the hall monitor Peaches, who was a large lady with curly blond hair and a ski pole that she used to point at people and say, "GET TO CLASS."

We avoided all of them and Berkeley was safely at the boxes we'd made into a desk.

"I'll be back after my second class."

"Okay," she said. She was pulling out the circus tickets and her crayons and her scissors, like this was normal. Like this was where she belonged and for a brief moment, I saw how good she was. How she was willing to do anything for me and Mom.

I gave her a kiss on her head and she said, "Can you get me more paper?"

"Sure," I said.

And then I left.

CHAPTER 66

All through class I was filled with love for my sister.

I was going to take care of her.

I was going to fix this.

I was going to get Dad.

I'd find Bart at lunch. I'd find him. And we'd go to Bryce. And if he couldn't go, I could ask Carlene now. Carlene was my friend. Bart and Carlene. One of them would come with me and we'd get Dad. And Dad would come. And he'd help Mom. And everything would be okay. I'd be okay. Berk would be okay. Maybe we'd even have a circus.

In English we were talking about similes and I wrote down, "Berkeley is like the sun, warm and bright." It was dumb but it was how I felt.

In math, I drew a picture of a part dragon, part dog. I knew she'd like it. I even shaded the dog's face with a pink pen I found in my backpack.

When the bell rang after math, I ran to take her my drawing and drop off more scrap paper that I got from math. I wanted to tell her I loved her and that I had a plan. And even if the plan didn't work, school was going to be out in two weeks. Two more horrible weeks and then we'd ride bikes to the rec center every day and I'd go down the waterslide and I'd take her to the park and we'd read books and play on the tramp.

I ran to tell her all that and when I opened the door to the storage closet, saying BERK!

I froze.

Like a bad dream, my little sister was gone.

CHAPTER 67

Steve Fossett was not always successful.

It all started when he was a Boy Scout and he went on a fifty-mile hike.

He didn't think he could do it.

He thought he was going to die and he cried and cried and cried.

I don't know if he really cried but I know he said it was hard.

But he told himself, keep going. Keep going. One more day. One more footstep.

And by the end of the week, blisters and swollen toes and mosquito bites and sunburn later, he was at the top of a mountain.

"Never give up," he says in his memoir. Never give up. Even if it's just a fifty miler with a bunch of Boy Scouts.

Or a missing sister who you promised you'd never let down.

Never give up, said the best adventurer in the world.

CHAPTER 68

I sat in the office.

Mom was in with the principal and a social worker and I hadn't seen Berk.

"Where is she?" I asked the secretary.

"Who?"

"My sister?"

"I don't know," she said.

"You don't know? How can you not know?"

She looked at me. And then she looked at the other secretary who looked at the student secretary and why were there so many secretaries? And why didn't any of them know anything?

"I'm sure she's fine," one of them said, the second one.

They didn't know what they were talking about. No one knew what they were talking about.

I stood up.

I sat back down.

I stood up again.

The student secretary who I knew was named Rudy, which was a stupid name, she said, "Are you okay?"

They were all watching me and I said, "Did you know a monkey can rip your face off?"

The girl's eyes got all big and I was like, "Oh yeah. Yours too." I said to the other secretary.

And then to the other one, "And yours for sure."

Then I said, "And you know what? I am done with all of this. I am done with all of this."

I climbed up on the front desk and the main lady was like, "Uh, you can't do that." And I said, "Oh I can't? I can't? I can't do this?"

And I kicked the stapler off.

Then I kicked the papers.

Then I kicked a pile of yellow papers. *Ahhhahhaha-hahhahahahaha!!!!!!!!!*

I suddenly knew what Grant felt when he'd gotten in a rage. I was kicking everything. I was jumping from table to desk to table and the student secretary was crying and the main secretary was calling Peaches and another kid who had clearly been sent to the principal's office came in and went right back out and then soon, the hall was filled with people.

There was Carlene and Bonnie and stupid Jared who called me a retard. There was Grant and Mrs. Sydney Gunnerson and Melody. There was Lala and Delilah and Paul with his UFC friends. And then there was my dumb-bum dad, holding hands with Bart.

I CAN DO WHATEVER I WANT. I CAN DO WHAT-
EVER I WANT AND I'LL KEEP DOING IT UNTIL YOU
TELL ME WHERE MY SISTER IS!

"Olivia.

"Olivia?"

The principal was looking at me.

I was sitting in the same chair.

The main secretary was typing something. Rudy, the
stupid student secretary, was stapling and listening to
her headphones, and the third one was watching me.

I closed my eyes. Please let me hold it together. Please
let me hold it together.

"Olivia," she said, "I've been talking to your mother."

My mother.

"And it seems that there are some problems at the
home right now."

The home.

"We are going to take some measures."

Measures.

I looked over. Mom was standing now, the social
worker talking in her ear. My mom bent over.

Then I had a thought.

Had Bart told on us?

Would he tell on us?

Maybe he did work for the FBI.

Or maybe Carlene.

Did Carlene tell on us?

Did she know? Did she see us walk into the building?

Did she have enough time? Would they act that fast?

Did one of my friends tell on us?

Was Mom going to jail?

Was *I* going to jail?

I'd once seen a reality TV show that followed around juvenile delinquents who all lived in a youth detention center together and they sat around in circles and talked about their problems and then went around with vests on picking up trash and one girl named Nina said she was going to be a doctor some day and all the other juvenile delinquents were like ha-ha. No way, you dumb-bum. You can't be a doctor. They look at your record when you apply for college and if you've been in juvie you can't do crap and she starts bawling and they have to take her away on a cart and I'm sure they do electric shock on her, though they don't show that, and when I asked Mom she said, "No, Olivia. No one does electric shock anymore," which I know is not true because I saw it in real life on another show.

But anyway, I might be going to jail. And getting electric shock therapy.

"Do you understand?" the principal was saying.

I looked at her.

"No."

"No?"

"No."

Mom came out.

The social worker came out.

Mom didn't look at me at first and the social worker said, "You're going to come with me, sweetheart."

I looked at her. "What? With you?"

"Just for a bit," she said. "We're going to go to a place that's really fun. Just for a bit."

"What about Berkeley?"

"Your sister's already there," she said.

That was good. That was good.

"Mom?" I said.

Mom said, "It's okay."

"What's okay?"

"Just go with her."

"Where are you going?"

"It'll be okay," Mom said. "I made a mistake."

The principal and the social worker nodded.

The secretary who was watching us but acting like she wasn't, actually all three secretaries were watching, they nodded.

My mom made a mistake.

I hated this place.

"It was my idea," I said. "This was my idea," I said to the lady. And then to the principal. "This was my idea.

My mom said no. We can't do this, take a little girl to middle school and I lied to her. I told her everyone brought their sisters to school. I was in charge of Berkeley. This was my idea."

The social worker and the principal gave each other looks. Looks that made me crazy.

I hated it when adults thought they were smarter than me. When they thought they were deep and I wasn't deep. When they thought they had a gut and I didn't have a gut.

When they thought they knew better when you know what? You know what? I know a whole lot fifty times better than all of you. I wanted to scream that. I wanted to scream at everyone.

I looked at Mom.

If she was not herself before, she was really not herself now.

The lady who just two days before had settled a neighborhood brawl and who Bart said was tough and Carlene said was cool, that lady was now standing there but not standing there. She was curled up on herself, her eyes glazed. Her hands shaking.

I was mad at her.

But I was also sad for her.

I wanted to do something.

To steal her and put her in my backpack.

Or hold her in my arms and sing "Rock-a-Bye Baby," and she would laugh and cry and I would say leave her alone.

Or tell her I was sorry. I was so sorry I let her down.

Then the lady, the social worker said to me, "We called your father. He's on his way."

CHAPTER 69

We called your father. He's on his way. Ha-ha-ha-ha-ha-ha-ha-ha-ha-ha-ha-ha-ha.

CHAPTER 70

The social worker lady named Jan said something cheerful, I didn't even hear it and she took my arm and we were walking out.

Mom was not walking out.

She was back there.

She was in the Dixon Middle School office.

I wondered if they'd lock her up in the supply closet.

Maybe she'd be trapped there for the rest of her life.

Maybe Dixon was jail.

Or maybe it was hell.

Maybe Mom was going to hell and maybe I was, too.

I wondered if there really was a hell.

I wondered if there was a heaven.

I wondered if you could end up in heaven and know you were in the wrong place.

What if you didn't belong in heaven or hell? What if you belonged nowhere?

Would God let you just float in between?

Just let you be no one?

Nowhere?

Nothing?

Jan kept chattering and chattering and chattering. Springtime. Flowers. Fun times. Family. Won't be long. Your daddy. Teddy bears! Happy times. Swimming. Summer.

I looked at her.

Her mouth was moving still but I heard nothing.

And Dad was coming.

Ha-ha-ha-ha-ha-ha-ha-ha-ha-ha.

He had answered his phone. Or answered an email. Or answered a letter.

And he was coming.

We walked out into the gray.

She pointed to her car, which was red. Bright red, like a cherry.

I stared at it.

"Come on," she said. "It goes really fast."

I remember her saying that.

It goes really fast.

We were walking toward it. She was talking again.

And then I saw him.

He was standing across the street.

He wore a yellow tank top and puffy jeans. His hair a Mohawk.

He watched us. I watched him. Was he going to beat up Jan? Take me to Morocco?

He walked across the street and right before I got in

the car he said, "I'm so sorry. I'm so sorry. I couldn't let you do it."

My heart dropped and I was going to throw up.

He did tell.

Not Carlene.

Him.

He did.

Bart told.

I knew I'd never love anyone again.

He said, "Olivia. You have to understand."

And I said, "No."

CHAPTER 71

Jan and I sat in a room with three other people.

One was Berkeley, who was playing dolls with a little boy named Ace.

When I came in, I thought she'd run to me. I thought she'd cry and I'd cry and we'd hug and then I'd tell her I'm so sorry. I'm so sorry.

And then she'd hit me.

And it would hurt but then we would hug and Jan the social worker and all her coworker social workers would say, "Now there's some sisters who stick together."

But instead, when I walked in, Berkeley didn't look up.

I said, "Berkeley!"

And she and the boy started laughing about something.

"Berkeley?"

She glanced at me and waved and then went back to playing.

In that moment I felt exhausted. But mad. But exhausted.

Jan put her hand on my shoulder and said, "Let her play. She's been through something traumatic."

Barf. But true. But barf.

I sat down on a soft chair.

"Do you want a soda? Some crackers? An apple?"

"Yes," I said.

She brought me a Sprite and some Chicken in a Biskit and a Granny Smith, which I hate because they're so sour.

I sat there with all that on my lap.

I knew I should be thinking about what was going to happen next.

What Berk and I should do.

Would Dad come?

What should I say?

What should Berk say?

What would Mom say?

I knew I should be making a plan.

But instead, I put my head back on the chair, and fell asleep.

....

Dear Mom,

  They told me that you are going to stay
with Aunt Susan in Wisconsin for a while. Is
that true? I didn't think that would be true
because you haven't talked to her in so long.
If it is true, can I come visit? Are you okay?
According to the internet, you only have to
stay away for forty-eight hours. Can you come
back in forty-eight hours?

  Dad is here.

  There was a hearing and I told them it was
all my fault. They said you weren't in jail. They
said it would be okay. I told them it was all my
fault. I told Dad, too.

  I'm sorry I messed up.

                          Love, Olivia

....

When Dad brought us home, everyone was looking out their windows and watching. You could feel it.

Chip came over and fist-bumped Dad and they talked on the porch.

Carlene waved from her house and I waved back.

Delilah came over and said, "Where's LeAnn?" and Dad gave her a look like don't talk about that right now in front of the girls but she should talk about it.

I wanted her to talk about it.

But instead she said, "Okay, okay. I understand." Then she looked at me and Berk and said, "You all should come over and watch some *Iron Chef* later."

And I said, "Yes, please."

And Berk said, "Okay."

But Dad didn't let us.

And Melody got up off the steps and yelled over to me. She yelled, "Olivia!" and I waved.

And Dad waved, too.

Later there were cookies on our steps with a note that said FOR OLIVIA AND BERKELEY.

And Randy gave Dad a key because Dad lost his and

Bob and Grant talked to Dad about his new car because he had a new car.

Even Mrs. Sydney Gunnerson came over and asked if we were going to help her with her sale on Saturday, looking at Dad the whole time.

Everyone was so so happy to see him.

When we got inside Dad said, "Sit."

So we sat.

Then he said, "I have a lot of important things to tell you."

And I said, "I almost came to Bryce to find you."

He looked at me. "What?"

"I almost came to get you. At Bryce. We needed you."

He looked all concerned and said, "Oh, honey. I wasn't at Bryce Canyon."

Wasn't.

At.

Bryce.

Canyon.

Wasn't.

At.

Bryce.

Canyon.

Wasn't.

At.

Bryce.

Canyon.

I stood up.

I clenched my fists.

I was about to scream but then a police officer named Biff knocked on the door and said, "I'm sorry. I'm going to arrest this man." And Dad said, "What are you talking about? What's happening?" And he looked at me. "What's happening, Olivia?"

And I shrugged and Berk shrugged and the police said, "I now arrest you for being the biggest fattest liar dad on the biggest fattest liar planet."

And then Dad, he started sobbing and sobbing and I said, "Don't eat the spaghetti," because I'd heard they do gross things to Italian foods in prison and then they took him away in a police car.

But really, he sat next to me and said, "Oh, honey. I wasn't at Bryce Canyon."

And I tried to breathe.

Breathe.

Breathe.

He wasn't in Bryce Canyon. He was in Salt Lake City, which is forty minutes from here.

Forty minutes.

I sat there.

"Do you want to move in with me?" he said. "Maybe just until we get things figured out?"

I sat there.

Berk sat there.

Salt Lake City.

Forty minutes away.

And . . .

He looked different.

He wore a suit.

He had no goatee.

He was thinner.

He was serious.

He lived in Salt Lake City.

Forty minutes from here.

"No," I said.

Berkeley held my hand.

He squatted in front of us. "Look. I was going to come back. I always meant to come back. It's just, things got complicated."

I watched his face. It had wrinkles.

He stood up. Paced around a bit.

"Your mom said you needed time to adjust. I was traveling."

Adjust to what? Mom said we needed to adjust? Didn't sound like Mom.

He kept talking. He liked to talk. He told us things about things and then more things. And he's sorry and then there's things and my mom said things and he said things and there are things. And he meant to do this and he meant to do that and things. And he didn't always live so close. He just moved back. He'd been in recovery. We don't know what that means but it's important and he'll explain it someday. It's not what we think. Not at all what we think. It's just. It's just. Someday when we're older. When we can understand. In fact in fact in fact. He has a great condo and things. There are things. He was planning on coming to get us for a weekend. We should talk more. About things. Lots of things. Things things.

Then he said, "I think we should all move to Salt Lake. There are kids around. There's a park pretty close."

His face was so big. Was it always so big?

I said, "No."

He looked at me. "Olivia. It's not really up for discussion."

I stared at him.

Then he started pacing again. "The only problem is the condo is small. I could make room for you girls but you need to finish out school and I have to work and it's a new job but I might be able to make it permanent if I do well."

Do well.

Do well.

Do well.

Then he says "Mom. Mom, LeAnn is fine. She's always fine."

He looked at me. "Your mother is fine, right? This was all a mistake."

I didn't say anything.

He lived in Salt Lake City.

Forty minutes away.

He sat across from us on the ripped-up recliner. Took a breath for the first time home. Took a breath and looked around. "You girls didn't change a thing."

And he was right. We still had his football trophies on a shelf. We still had his poster of the sunset in Hawaii up on the wall. The same blankets. The same rugs. The same sayings on the fridge.

Mom even still had the few clothes he left hanging in the closet.

Like our whole existence had been on hold, waiting for him to come home.

Suddenly I didn't want to be in there anymore.

He was talking about something but I didn't want to hear it.

I stood up.

Berkeley stood up.

"We're going to the tramp," I said.

"What tramp?"

"The trampoline outside."

"We have a trampoline?"

"No. You don't have a trampoline," I said. "*We* have a trampoline."

I took Berkeley's hand and we went outside in the sun, which is warm and bright.

CHAPTER 73

I go to school the next day.

Berkeley stays home with Dad, which feels weird to say. Or think.

I told Berkeley she didn't have to.

She could stay with Delilah or Melody or even Mrs. Sydney Gunnerson but she said it was okay.

"I want to be with Daddy."

"Are you sure?" I asked her. She doesn't understand. She doesn't get it.

"Yes," she said, her face fresh from a good night of sleep. "He said we could go on a bike ride."

So she's staying with him and I feel mad at her but also not mad at her because I want to go on a bike ride too but not really.

He is taking two weeks off from work until I finish school. He has to go to social services and he and Mom are going to blah blah blah blah figure it out blah blah blah blah blah.

Before I go, he and Berk eat breakfast and I say, "Did you get my emails?"

He says, "What emails?"

I say, "I emailed you."

He says, "Which email?"

And I say, "Your email account."

He says, "Oh, baby girl, I've had a new email address for ages."

I say, "Have a fun day!"

CHAPTER 74

And now I'm at school.

People are laughing.

Carlene says, "Hey, Olivia."

I say, "Hey."

Then she walks away with Bonnie.

I walk to my class.

I sit in English. People are doing a project. I am supposed to be doing a project.

I sit there.

It's so fun for everyone because school is almost out. I turn in my packet at the end of the class. The teacher says, "Good job." She says I probably won't have to go to summer school.

I say, "I want to go to summer school."

She says, "You do?"

I say, "Yes."

She says, "Why?"

I say, "Never mind."

I go to math.

Jared, the boy who called me a retard, says, "Your shirt is dumb."

I say, "Thank you."

He says, "You're welcome."

I listen to the teacher. He says that we have a test. He asks if there are any questions.

I say, "I have a question."

And he says, "What is that, Olivia?"

And I say, "Why is everyone in the world so crappy to each other."

People laugh.

Mr. Brown tells people to be quiet. Then he says to me, "What do you mean, Olivia?"

I say, "Why do people treat each other like crap?"

He says, "They don't always."

I say, "Don't they?"

He says, "Sometimes but not always."

Someone says, "No one treats me like crap."

Someone says to him, "You suck."

People start laughing.

I say, "I hate everyone."

People get quiet. Someone says, "Check and see if she has a shotgun."

Mr. Brown says, "Can I talk to you in the hall."

I say, "Sure."

In the hall he says, "Are you okay?"

I say, "No."

He says, "Do you want to talk to Miss Hill?"

I say, "No."

He says, "What do you want to do?"

I say, "I want to do nothing."

He says, "You want to do nothing?"

I say, "I want to be nothing."

He says, "This worries me."

I say, "Don't be worried."

He says, "Why?"

And I say, "Because it doesn't matter. Nothing I do matters."

He says, "I understand you are having some home issues."

I say, "I understand you have bad hair."

He laughs.

I don't laugh.

He says, "Let me take you down to Miss Hill's office for now and then I want to talk to you. I have prep period after this."

I say, "I know you do."

He says, "You know I do?"

And I say, "Yes, because last time you kept me after and you said I was smart."

He says, "That's right."

Then I say, "You are a liar."

I never talk like this to people like this. Or people like anything. But I can't stop myself.

He stares at me. Then he says, "Let's go down to Miss Hill's office for a bit."

I say, "Fine."

We walk down the hall.

I look in the classrooms as we go.

In one classroom I see Bart.

Bart sees me.

I want to throw a car in his face.

Mr. Brown says, "Do you know someone in there?"

I say, "No."

He says, "Do you have friends?"

I say, "No."

He says, "I'm worried about you."

I say, "I'm worried about you."

He says, "Here's Miss Hill's office."

I say, "Thank you."

He says, "I'm taking you in."

I say, "I can take myself in."

He says, "Okay."

I say, "Okay."

He walks back down the hall. I stand outside Miss Hill's office. He turns and looks at me.

I smile and wave at him. He says, "I'm going to come talk to you after my class."

I say, "Please do that."

He says, "Go in."

I say, "I need some time."

He says, "I can respect that."

I say, "The people in our class have probably destroyed the room."

He says, "You're right."

He turns and jogs down the hall.

I wait until he is gone.

I do not go in Miss Hill's office.

Instead I go up the stairs, around the corner, down the hall, and into the supply closet.

....

Dear Mom,

How are you? I'm great!

I have really been having a fun time at school. Only five days left! One of my teachers, Mr. Brown, he is so nice! He has decided that I need a special friend to go with me to all my classes. The special friend is a girl named Brenda who is very positive and is on student council! She thinks I'm special, too! She gets to help me with my homework during lunch and I stay after school and she makes sure I'm getting everything done! Mr. Brown and Miss Hill have arranged the whole thing! It's so nice to have people looking after me every second of every day.

Also, they have locked up the room that Berkeley used to hang out in. It's too bad because it's so nice in there. With couches and fun toys and a good atmosphere. I told them they should make it a lounge for people like me! They said they'd consider it!

Dad has come to the school a few times! He even came to class with me one day! He left Berkeley with Delilah, no problem! I no longer talk to my friend Bart. You remember him? He used to come sit with me and Berk on the tramp and he told me he was someone important but it turns out he is just a regular person at my school who does water aerobics and wears stupid clothes and hates school. Anyway, we decided that since I'm focused on my schoolwork and everything, we should take a break from ever talking to each other. It's a good feeling to get rid of people in your life who make you feel not special inside! Miss Hill told me that. I like it!

Anyway, Dad told me you aren't supposed to have contact with us yet. I told him Oh no! That's not right! On the internet it says you only have to stay away forty-eight hours! I emailed you about that! But Dad said it was special circumstances and you might not even be getting my emails! And he said, I'm so sorry. I said, that's okay! I'm still going to send them anyway!

No one is telling me or Berk what is going to happen but that's okay. We're just kids! We don't care!

Love you tons!

Olivia,
your daughter

....

CHAPTER 75

I sat on the tramp.

Berkeley was inside with Dad making Saturday chocolate chip waffles.

"Remember how I used to make these?" he said.

"No, I don't remember," I'd said, even though I did remember. I remembered how they weren't dry and crumbly like Mom's. I remembered how he knew how to put just the right amount of syrup in each little square. And I remembered how he would sit with us and tell us stories about when his dad made him chocolate chip waffles when he was a kid.

"You really don't remember?"

"Nope."

So I sat outside on the tramp, the sun hotter than it had been in weeks. I was trying not to be mad at Berk. Trying not to wish she were out here with me.

The summer was here, usually my favorite time in the whole world. But this year, it meant that school was almost out and if whatever needed to be figured out with Mom wasn't figured out and we would be moving with Dad up to Salt Lake City where we would sleep on his couch and maybe a lady across the hall could watch us while he went to work and then we could get Chinese takeout. Does that sound fun?

The Chinese takeout actually did sound fun but other than that, I was not excited about the end of school.

Bart had come over one day. Even knocked on the door.

My dad had answered and Bart said, "Can I talk to Olivia?"

And Dad had said, "Who are you?"

And he said, "Harrison."

And then Berk said, "Hi, Bart."

And Bart said, "Hi, Berkeley."

And Dad said, "I thought you said your name was Harrison." And Bart said, "It's complicated," and I was on my bed with my feet on the wall listening and even though I hate Bart with a passion, I liked hearing him talk to my dad about his names.

"Why is it complicated," Dad said.

"I can't tell you," Bart said.

"You can't tell me?"

"Nope."

It was quiet then and Berkeley said, "Do you have any candy."

And he said, "Yes," and Dad said, "Don't take candy from this kid."

And Berkeley said, "He's our friend," and Dad said, "He's not your friend if he can't tell me his real name," and Bart said, "It's Harrison." And Dad said, "Not Bart?"

And he said, "It's Bart also."

And Dad said, "I don't know what game you're trying to play."

And Bart said, "Can I talk to Olivia?"

And Dad said, "OLIVIA!"

And I said, "Not here."

And Dad said, "She's not here."

And Bart said, "Yes she is."

And Dad acted like he knew me and cared about me and he said, "You'll stay away from my daughter," and then I came running in and I said, "Don't you dare talk to my friend like that. He may have called the social services on Mom, but he has been here for us but not really, but more than you."

And Dad was shocked and I said, "Bart, go away."

And I said to Dad, "Dad, go away."

And then I said to Berk, "Go with me."

And I took her hand and we went outside and Melody had a hot-air balloon and Mrs. Sydney Gunnerson said, "Take this," and she handed me my favorite Italian baby doll in her entire collection and Berkeley and I climbed into the hot-air balloon and I smiled and everyone came out, including Grant and Bob.

And then I said, "That boy over there," because Bart and Dad stood on the front step, "that boy over there is spying on you for no good reason."

And Grant said, "Thank you for that information. It is very useful," and I said, "You're welcome."

And Melody said, "I'll reverse perm your hair" and I said, "I don't need a perm anymore."

And Carlene said, "What about the Monster Jam?"

And I said, "I'm going to start my own Monster Jam."

And Bart said, "What about how we were going to go to every state?"

And Berkeley and I will be sailing away and I said, "That's what we're doing right now, fat face."

And then the two of us, with cookies and happiness and rainbows and a hot tub will float into the clouds in our balloon shaped like a gigantic pig.

But then Bart said, "Tell her I came by."

And Dad said, "I will not tell her you came by until you tell me your real name."

And I put my legs straight up in the air and tried to touch my toes and I couldn't, which was really disappointing.

So even though Bart and I were through, I still sat on the tramp and kept track of old Grant, because I had nothing better to do and I had started to like watching him because he was so weird and because he hugged my mom and my mom talked to him about love which meant he had a broken heart and this was interesting to me.

Today he was on the phone with someone.

He was walking back and forth in front of his trailer, talking loudly and using his free arm to wave around.

I wrote down the words I heard:

Aching

Unfair

Toothpaste

Kiss

No

Yes

Please

Please

Please

Please

Sorry

I

Understand

No

Kitties

Yes

Chance

Last
Time
Please
No
No
NO
NO
Legs
Rhubarb
Applebees
Deodorant
Cheez Whiz
Love you
Forgive
Please
Dogs

It was a fascinating conversation.

Bob came out near the end of Grant's phone call and said, "We have to go."

Grant waved his arm at Bob.

Bob flipped him off.

Grant flipped him off.

Then they were flipping each other off together at the same time, which really made me feel warm inside.

~

Then Grant got off the phone.

They both got in the truck and drove away.

I lay back on the tramp.

I was getting sunburned.

Then suddenly Dad and Berk were in my face.

"We're going to the pool and then McDonald's and then Zurchers to get decorations for the circus," Berk was saying. Dad smiled. She'd told him about the stupid circus.

I said, "No thanks."

And he said, "You've been out here too long. Berk told me you usually go swimming on Saturdays. Run in and get changed."

Then they were getting in his fancy new car and I was sitting up.

I looked at my watch. It was the exact same time as last time.

And Bart. Who I hated. Who betrayed me. Bart was at the pool.

Even though I did *not* want to go, I also very much wanted to go.

I went and put on my swimsuit, grabbed my Grant notebook, and ran to the car.

CHAPTER 76

My notebook was almost full.

All my notes on Grant.

All the sweepstakes or contests I had ever entered.

The Monster Jam dates.

All my observations.

Everything I had found out about Steve Fossett.

There were other things in there, too.

When Bart told me about the Mason-Dixon Line I started doing research. If he and I went on a road trip when we were older and married or not married, whatever, we could follow the exact route of Charles Mason and Jeremiah Dixon who surveyed the line.

This was before I hated Bart's guts.

I'd made a list of things we'd need to bring.

A tent.

Sleeping bags.

We'd need a phone.

I'd never seen Bart with a phone, which was weird. Of everyone in the whole world he and I were the only two people over eight who didn't have one.

But if we were going to every state in the United States, we'd need a GPS thing.

Or I guess a map.

I found a stove that would fit in the pocket of a backpack that could heat up soup or chili or hot chocolate.

We'd need clothes and boots and we'd need some money but not a lot.

I'd also made a list of things we could talk about because sometimes my parents, before Dad left, didn't talk a lot.

Things We Could Talk About:
Birds
Hair
FBI things
Halloween costumes for our kids
Names of kids
Cookies
Countries we wanted to go see
Wild animals that had been known to rip people's faces off
Funny movies we would've already watched together
Funny movies we wanted to watch together
Why people wear clothes that are too tight
Chest hair
God
Music
Stupid people

Daylight saving time

Volcanoes—Mt. Vesuvius

Ghosts

Teeth

Cookie jars

What does Obi-Wan do the whole time Luke Skywalker is growing up?

Why someone can use the same recipe and the cookies taste bad

His family

Not my family

Space travel

Body odor

Underwater caves, danger of

Haunted Houses, danger of

Kids

Houses

Divorce, how we would never

Tater Tots

Fancy things we wanted to do together for the rest of our lives

The first page of the notebook I had colored with Berk's colored pencils my favorite saying from all the contests I entered: YOU MAY ALREADY BE A WINNER.

I stared at it as we drove to the rec center.

~

Dad was talking loud on his phone to someone about insurance. He promised whoever it was, they would not be disappointed. He was going to be back in the office in one week but anything they needed could be done online.

He promised.

He promised.

He promised.

Berkeley held my hand. Tight. My sweet little sister, her suit on, her goggles adjusted, her towel around her neck.

I was going to rip out the lists other than the Grant information from the notebook but then I didn't. We pulled into the parking lot and Dad was still talking.

We got out.

He sat there.

We waited.

He was talking with his hands now.

We stood there.

Still talking.

"I want to go in," Berk said.

"Me too," I said.

I took her hand and we walked into the rec center like we always did.

CHAPTER 77

"Should we wait for Daddy?" Berk asked, but she was walking faster than me, almost pulling me along.

We stopped to show our passes and I looked back. Dad had finally gotten out and was coming but he was also talking to a lady.

A pretty lady with red hair and a nice face and yoga pants and she laughed and Dad laughed and I thought I might throw up.

I thought I might throw up right then all over the rec center desk and the boy with the name tag Brad would say, "Disgusting," and I'd say, "You know what's disgusting?" And I'd throw up more and more and more and Dad would come running in and the lady would come in, too, and she'd say, "What's wrong with her," and he'd say, "I don't know."

And, I'd say, "You do know! You do know you big butt-head piece of butt face." And he'd be shocked but also he'd know, he'd know because just like me, between his big and little intestines, right in that itty-bitty space, he has a gut and that gut would be giving him a feeling and even if he wanted to ignore it, even if he wanted to smile at the redhead and say, "I am so sorry my daughter called me a butthead piece of butt face. I have no idea why she is throwing up all over the rec center," even though he might want to say that, he wouldn't be able to because he'd know the truth. And the truth was, he was not who he said he was.

He left us.

He left us alone.

He left Mom.

He left Berk.

He left me.

We walked to the pool area. Dad followed us.

The lady with the yoga pants did not come with him and I said a prayer that said: Thank you.

Instead of going to the girls' locker room, we went to the family one.

I found a locker.

"Aren't you changing?" I asked him.

He was wearing a tight T-shirt and tight jeans and leather flip-flops. I didn't understand him. He never wore stuff like that before. He wore Bermuda shorts and Hawaiian shirts and maybe flip-flops but one dollar ones from Old Navy.

He said, "I'm not getting in, girls."

Berkeley looked at him. "You're not?"

"Nah. I don't think so."

"You have your suit. I saw you put your suit in," she said.

"Yeah, but I need to do some work." He held up his phone.

We both stared at him. It was loud in there. It's always loud in there. He was going to try to talk on the phone?

"You can't do work in here," I said.

"Sure I can."

Berkeley was quiet.

"It's too loud."

"And I want you to go down the slide with me," she said.

"Maybe in a minute," he said. "I'll just go sit over there." He pointed to the tables and chairs out of the pool area. Like all the way out on the other side of the glass by the entrance. He was leaving. He was going to sit out there and leave us.

"You watch Berk, Olivia. It'll be fine."

It'll be fine.

It'll be fine.

It'll be fine.

That's when something inside me burst.

It was sudden, like a firecracker.

Like a firecracker that everyone thinks is a dud at first. A total and complete dud.

You wait and you wait and it keeps not going off.

You keep waiting.

And waiting.

And then someone says, "It's a dud," and you think no, it's not a dud. Give it time. Give it time to heat up.

Just wait.

And then it doesn't happen. It sits there and people start to get bored and they look at the other firecrackers and some people get up to get more Cheetos and they start to forget about the firecracker.

They forget about it until *BAM BAM BAM BAM BAM* FIRE AND *BAM* PEOPLE JUMP AWAY AND *BAMBAM-BAM*. SOMEONE IS BURNED. IS SOMEONE BURNED? SCREAMING SCREAMING! CALL THE AMBULANCE. *BAM BAM BAM BAM BAM*. IT'S THE BIGGEST FIRE-CRACKER ANYONE HAS EVER SEEN. NO ONE EXPECTED A FIRECRACKER OF THIS MAGNITUDE!!!!

I went *BAM!*

I went: *BAM BAM BAM BAM BAM*.

I went *BAM BAM BAM* in real life. In my real life.

I went: I AM NOT WATCHING BERK! I AM NOT. YOU GET IN YOUR SWIMSUIT. YOU GET IN YOUR SWIMSUIT AND YOU GO DOWN THE SLIDE WITH HER!

I went: NOW. DO IT NOW.

I went: SCREAMING. MY BLOOD RUSHING. MY HEART POUNDING.

He stared at me. I thought he was going to get mad. I wanted him to get mad I think. I wanted him to yell back but instead all the butthead did was say, "Are you okay?"

I was breathing breathing breathing. Try to calm down. Try to calm down down down. Try. Try. Try. And then it all came spewing up again.

And I went: NO NO NO I AM NOT OKAY I AM NOT OKAY! I AM NOT DOING THIS I AM NOT DOING ANYTHING I AM DOING NOTHING.

People stared at me. An old man with lots of hair took a step toward me and I realized I didn't know what I was saying and Dad was red-faced and Berkeley was looking at the ground and I finally said I AM GOING TO SWIM LAPS IN THE COMPETITION POOL. I'LL SEE YOU IN AN HOUR. DON'T TALK TO ME EVER AGAIN.

And then I twirled around fast, faster than I was expecting and felt a little sick, and then stomped off, out of the kid pool area, around the bend and then right into the competition pool without looking back.

CHAPTER 78

Bart was there.

He was in the pool with five hundred fat ladies and an old man with a bald head. When he saw me he waved and that's when I started bawling.

....

Dear Mom,

I tried Aqua Zumba today. I was the only one besides Bart, who is a boy I know, under fifty years old.

Bart told me normally he would never do water aerobics because it's for old people with fake hips but he had to because it's a good workout and it helps him train for Tae Kwon Do, which is not just karate but an ancient burial art that they did to help defend themselves from enemies who were interested in disturbing their peace.

He said he would avoid using the force in real life unless there was a genuine threat. He is a purple belt, which is two levels below black but he's only that because his sensei said he should slow down because if you move too fast, you get a target on your back. I'm not sure what that means. It's also required for the FBI apparently. They don't let people know how cardio-vascularly fit you can get doing water aerobics.

I don't know if you know this but he's also going to run a hundred miles. I might do it with him.

Dad went down the slides with Berkeley. They also did the rock-climbing wall in the deep end and Berkeley made him stand in the kiddie pool on the X so she could spray him with water.

I stopped typing.

I didn't want Mom to think I liked Dad better than her. Or that he was doing a nicer job than she was because I *made* him do that. I *made* him get in and he was talking to that dumb-bum redhead.

So I put.

He is always on his phone and he doesn't know the lyrics to any good songs like you do.

Please come home soon. He is boring.

Love, Olivia

....

When I started bawling on the deck of the competition pool, Bart got out. He was really there and there really was Aqua Zumba and I really did start to sob.

No one else noticed, thank you, not even the lifeguard who was a girl with a long face and her job is to save lives and I was about to die and she didn't even look over, but he did.

He got out and I almost went back to the locker room because I hate him and he said, "Olivia!" He said it loud but not too loud. I turned around and he was jogging up and dripping and he said, "What's wrong?"

And I should have said, "I'm mad at you," but instead I said, "My butthead dad."

And he said, "Your dad is here?"

And I said, "Yeah."

And he said, "Where?"

And I pointed through the glass where Dad was standing there watching. He wasn't coming after me. He was just standing there.

"Is something wrong with him?" Bart said.

"What?"

"What's wrong with him? He looks weird."

I looked at Dad. His stupid cool clothes. His hair sticking straight up with a gallon of gel. And his face all fake concerned. He did look weird.

"Yes," I said. "Something is very wrong with him."

Dad motioned for me to come back.

I looked at Bart. "I hate him," I said, wiping my nose.

Bart said, "He was rude when I came over."

I said, "I know."

And he said, "But I thought you liked him. I thought he worked for the Parks Department and maybe the NSA."

I looked over again. Berk was dragging Dad back to the locker room, probably to make him put on his suit. He waved for me to come.

Bart said, "What are you going to do?"

I stared at Dad's face.

"Do you want me to go beat him up?" Bart asked, and I smiled.

Then I looked at the ladies and one old guy jumping around in the pool.

I looked at the blond middle-aged woman on the deck in Zumba clothes.

I looked at the boom box or whatever they call those, blasting Cher.

They looked ridiculous.

And happy.

And I said, "Can I do what you're doing?"

And he said, "Water Zumba?"

I said, "Please."

And he said, "Are you serious?"

I said, "Please."

And he said, "It can be dangerous."

I said, "I'll risk it."

So that's how I did my first Aqua Zumba class.

CHAPTER 80

Everyone seemed to know the music and Mrs. Sydney Gunnerson really was in the class and was pretty much the best. Twirling in the water, looking over her shoulder at just the right time. Clapping her hands to the beat.

She waved at me and I waved back at her.

No wonder she always closed her Antique Dolls and Collectibles shop at exactly eleven o'clock on the dot. She had to get to aerobics.

But I was bad at it.

When I was supposed to turn, I didn't turn and when I wasn't supposed to turn I did.

I was off every single song.

"It takes practice," Bart said at one point, and I said, "I can't believe how hard it is."

He said, "I know. Navy Seals do this to train."

I laughed.

The only time I caught on was when they were cooling down with stretches.

But one good thing: I laughed a lot. And for maybe five seconds I forgot about Dad. And Mom.

Then afterward, when we got out of the pool, the instructor came up to us, sweat was dripping off her shoulders. She should have jumped in the pool.

She had a weathered face, brown from the sun, bleached blond hair in a ponytail, and a tight tank top that showed the rolls on her stomach, which clearly she didn't care if they showed.

"Who's your friend?" she said to Bart, handing him a towel.

He seemed nervous all of a sudden.

"She's from school," he said.

The woman looked at me. "You're from school?"

"Uh," I said. "Yeah?"

She examined me, I don't know why.

"I'm glad he has a friend from school. Maybe he'll stop ditching so much." She bumped into Bart who blushed.

Then she said, "What's your name?"

"Olivia."

"Hi, Olivia."

She stuck out her hand, "I'm Roxi."

"Hi, Roxi," I said.

She looked at Bart. Bart was rubbing his head with the towel, not looking at us.

Then she said, "You should come over to the house sometime."

"Mom," Bart said, "stop."

It was his mom.

And she said, "I think you should marry my son."

And I said, "What?"

And Bart said, "What?"

And his mom said, "Don't be silly. I can see the love between you two."

And I said, "No. We just met. We're too young."

And I looked at Bart and even though I knew he thought it was crazy, too, I also saw that there was something in his eye. Something like a twinkle. Maybe it could last. Maybe we wouldn't end up in the trailer park with lots of trophies and no jobs and sad kids.

And he said, "I do love you."

And I said, "You do?"

And he said, "I'll take care of you."

And I said, "I don't need you to."

And he said, "You don't?"

And I said, "No."

And he said, "What do you need?"

And I said, "A friend."

And he said, "I am your friend."

And his mom said, "Gary, come here."

And an enormous man with a tattoo of a bulldog on his belly came dripping over.

"Will you marry these two?" she said.

"Right now?" I gasped.

"Right now," Bart said.

And his mom smiled. "Sometimes you just know."

So we were married. And everyone cheered and they threw cotton candy at us and Bart said, "We will live in Paris," and I said, "We will?"

And he said, "Yes. And Hamburg. And Istanbul. And Hong Kong. And we'll never come back."

And I said, "What about Berk?"

And he said, "Berk can come, too!"

And then I said, "Yes! Let's go to Mongolia!" And then I took his face and I kissed him soft and as romantic as I could and there were real fireworks and crying and it was the best day of my life.

CHAPTER 81

His mom laughed. Then she said, "Olivia, you should come to our house for dinner."

And even though it wasn't marriage, which I didn't want anyway, it was something.

Bart said, "She can't."

I said, "I can't?"

And he said, "Can you?"

I said, "I think I can."

Then he said, "She might be able to."

And I said, "I can."

And he said, "Are you sure? What about your dad?"

I said, "What about him?"

And he said, "Would he let you?"

I said, "I don't know."

He said, "She probably can't."

I said, "I probably can."

His mom folded her arms, smiling.

Then he said, "You probably can?"

I said, "Yes."

And his mom said, "It's settled then. We grill at six."

Then someone walked up to her to ask her a question.

Bart looked at me. "You don't have to come."

He had no idea that inside I was jumping up and down. I was screaming. I was more excited than I had ever been in my whole life except for the time we went to Disney when I was six.

I said, "I can come."

And he said, "She cooks bad food."

I said, "I don't care."

And he said, "Okay."

And I said, "Okay."

I couldn't read his face. Why didn't he want me to come?

He started to say something and I knew it was going to be that I couldn't come because he didn't like me. But instead he said, "I would never do Aqua Zumba in real life but it's good for Tae Kwon Do."

His lips were smooth like he wore a Chapstick regularly which is a good idea. Plus, he had braces. I'd always wanted braces.

Finally, he stopped talking and said, "I have to go."

I said, "What?"

And then I realized that the pool area was almost empty except for a few lap swimmers, and his mom was waiting for him by the door.

"Oh," I said. "Yeah. Okay. Thanks."

And he said "Thanks?" Then he said, "I live at Nine Eleven North Elm Street."

Panic went all over my body.

"Where?"

"Nine-one-one North Elm."

I said it in my head 911 North Elm Street. 911 North Elm Street. 911 North Elm Street.

I knew I was going to forget it. I could not forget it.

Then he said, "Just remember, emergency Freddy Krueger."

And I said, "What?"

And he said, "Never mind."

Then he said, "What are you going to do now?"

I looked over at the play pools. Kids running around screaming. I looked at dumb-bum Dad. Ugh.

"I'm going to swim a few laps," I said.

"You are?" he said.

"Yeah," I said. "I do it all the time. I like it over here."

He said, "That's cool."

And I said, "Thank you."

And then he left. But not before his mom yelled, "See you tonight," and I said, "See you tonight," which sounded like I was copying her.

And then I stood there.

I got back in the pool and didn't swim any laps. Instead I waited for five minutes on the clock.

911 North Elm Street. 911 North Elm Street. 911 North Elm Street.

Emergency. North Freddy Krueger.

Then I got out and went to the kiddie pools where I belonged.

CHAPTER 82

Dad came into my room after we got home.

He said, "I need to talk to you, Livy."

And I said, "I don't need to talk to you."

I'd found him and Berkeley right away at the pool. They were on the pirate ship. Even Dad.

I sat in the shallow pool and acted like Dad was no one. Berk would yell to show me something in the water and I'd watch and laugh but when Dad tried to get me to look at him, no way.

He sprayed me with a huge cannon and I tried to act like I didn't notice which wasn't so easy if you want to know the truth.

We went to McDonald's after the pool, which was Mom's place and I ordered a salad, which was a pretty low blow but I didn't care. No way was I going to order something good and make him feel happy about himself.

So now he was in my room. Berk outside playing and I was busy looking at the ceiling.

"I know you're upset."

The ceiling.

"Olivia? Can we talk?"

I closed my eyes and tried to imagine what it would be like to live in an adobe house.

He sat down on the bed and did a sigh, a big old sigh like his life was hard. Like talking to redheads and arguing on the phone and having fancy apartments in the city that was not Bryce Canyon with no room for kids was hard.

"I'm sorry I left," he said.

I said, "Barf."

He said, "What?"

And I said, "Barf."

He said, "Barf?"

And I said, "Barf."

He did a face like I was so immature but I didn't care. Then he said, "Your mother and I were having some problems. I was having problems."

I stuck my fingers in my ears.

"Stop that," I think he said, but I wasn't sure because I couldn't hear him. "Stop that right now," he said, but again, I couldn't be too sure.

Then he reached over and yanked my fingers out of my ears.

"That was rude," I said.

"Was it?" he said. "Was that rude?" he said, his voice rising.

"Yeah," I said. "It was. Besides you already told me everything."

He sighed. Then he said, "No I didn't. Here's the thing. Your mother and I were so young when we got married."

I stuck my fingers in my ears again.

He pulled them out again and kept talking. "I made some mistakes. I . . ." he stopped.

"What mistakes," I asked.

He looked at me. "I'll tell you when you're older."

"Tell me now," I said.

He shook his stupid head. "You're too young."

"No, I'm not."

"You are," he said, and I could feel the tears start to come. He didn't know me. He didn't know me at all.

I said, "Did you get a girlfriend?"

His face got really red then but I didn't care. I didn't. "Did something happen with Melody?" I said.

"Who?"

"Melody, from down the street."

He stopped talking for a minute. Then he said, "Did your mother say that?"

"No. But Mom doesn't like her."

He sighed. "One time I said Melody was pretty. That's all. And your mother, she freaked out. You know how she can get."

I thought about that. I thought about Mom. My

mom. Her hands. So cold. Always so cold. And her arms. And her face. And her wrinkles. And her hair pulled tight. And her back. Her back that had held her up while she wiped down walls and scrubbed people's floors and vacuumed room after room after room.

I thought about how Mom could get and I wanted to scream.

Dad kept talking. "Like I was saying, we got married so young."

I felt sick. So sick I might throw up for real.

He kept going.

Mom has so many expectations and he tried he tried so so hard and us girls he loves us girls but it was too much and your mother, he knows it was hard for her but she knew it wasn't working and shouldn't be talking like this talking like this talking like this but I'm right, I am old now and I should hear the truth and he wants the best for me and I can always come to him and blah blah blah blah blah on and on and he's so sorry.

Finally, when eighty percent of my body was turned to stone, finally he said, "I'm so glad we could talk like this."

I said nothing. I was nowhere.

Then he said, "I love you, Livy, and like it or not, I'm here. And like it or not, we are going to have to make this work."

"No we don't."

He looked at me. "Yes we do."

"When's Mom coming home?"

"I don't know."

"You don't know?"

"I don't know."

I thought about Mom. How if it was me, if my husband who I loved and loved and loved, took a knife to my heart and left me and made up stupid excuses like we were too young and blah blah barfity blah, maybe I would crack down the middle, too.

But then, moms weren't allowed to crack.

It should be a law.

Because what about their kids?

What about me and Berk?

Weren't we someones?

I closed my eyes and tried so hard to hear a helicopter coming.

From far away I heard his voice. He said, "Can you please help me? Help me make this work?"

"No," I whispered.

"No?"

"No."

He was quiet.

Then he said, "I don't remember you being like this."

"Being like what?" I said.

"Stubborn," he said, rubbing his face.

My heart started thumping. He didn't remember me being like this? He didn't remember *me* being like this? I made a goal not to talk to him ever again for the rest of my life. But then I couldn't help it, I said, "I don't remember *you* being like this."

He looked at me. "Like what?"

I was about to say something like a butthead. You are a butthead. But then I knew that wasn't what I really wanted to say. What I wanted to say was so big, so huge, so gigantic, it wouldn't fit in this trailer. It wouldn't fit in this entire neighborhood. What I wanted to say could blow up the entire state of Utah, it was so big.

So instead I said, "I'm going to my friend Bart's house for dinner."

Dad looked at me. "What?"

I said it again.

He said, "When?"

I said, "Tonight."

He said, "He invited you to dinner?"

I said, "Yes."

He said, "I don't know his parents. And isn't his name Harrison?"

I said, "So."

And he said, "So I don't even know his name."

I said, "So."

He said, "So you can't go."

I said, "What?"

And he said, "You can't go."

I said, "What are you talking about?"

He said, "I don't think your mom would let you go."

"Yes, she would."

He sat for a minute.

Then he said, "Would she?"

"Yes," I said.

Then I thought about it, would she? I thought she would. Would she not?

Then I thought how she'd let me take Berkeley to school and how she definitely wouldn't care if I went to some stranger's house for dinner.

I said, "She'd let me go."

He looked at me. "Would she?" he said again.

"She would."

He stopped talking.

He looked at his hands.

Then he said, "Is she really okay?"

Is she okay? Was he talking about Mom? He was talking about Mom.

"Uh," I said. "No."

He nodded. "I know."

Then he said, "She told me she was fine. That she was working nights to maybe go to college. Be a nurse or some crap. I should have known she was lying." He paused.

Was that what she was saving for?

He kept going, talking more to himself than me. "I can't believe she let you take Berk to school with you." He sighed. "I'll call her."

"Call who?" I asked.

He looked at me. "Your mom."

He could call her?

He was just going to call her?

On the phone?

He could call her.

I said, "You can call her?" my voice hard to get out.

He looked at me funny. "Of course I can call her."

"What about the no contact."

He sighed. "That was only for a couple of days. Forty-eight hours but we decided she should take some time for herself, take a little break before she came back."

A break.

A break.

Take a little break.

Then he said, "I talked to her earlier."

He'd called her. He'd talked to her.

I swallowed. "In Wisconsin?"

He was tapping something on his phone. Distracted. "What?"

"Is she still in Wisconsin," I asked.

"She was," he said, not looking at me. "She's not any-more."

"Where is she now?"

"She's at a friend's house."

"What friend?" my blood pumping. Mom didn't have that many friends.

He ignored me. Started doing something on his phone.

"What friend?" I asked.

He didn't respond.

"Where is she, Dad?"

He set the phone down and took a big breath.

He turned his ring on his finger, which, why was he wearing that all of a sudden? He never wore it before.

"Where is she?"

He sighed. "I told her to give me a little more time. I told her to stay away."

"Where. Is. She."

He looked at me. "She's at Delilah's."

CHAPTER 83

I busted out the door.

"Olivia, stop," Dad said.

But I didn't stop.

The sun was still high in the sky and everyone was out.

I ran right down the street, past Carlene and dumb-bum Bonnie. Carlene said, "Olivia, wait," but I ignored her. Past Berk working on the circus with Sadie and Jane. Past Melody, who sat on her steps. Past Bob, who was doing something to his motorcycle with Grant and yelling at him to hand him a wrench. Past Mrs. Sydney Gunnerson's house where it smelled like burning bread. Past UFC Paul's trailer, where he probably wasn't home. All the way to the corner where Delilah lived.

I went right up the steps.

Pounded on the door.

Delilah, in her floral peacock T-shirt that she always wore and which Mom said was a crime against humanity, opened the door, Ruthanne jumping at her feet.

"Olivia!" she said. So surprised! So surprised! "What are you doing here?"

I pushed past her into the trailer where there she was.

My mom.

Sitting on the couch.

Watching a TV show. *Chopped.*

Like it was any other old day.

She stood up.

I felt tears about to burst and I didn't want them to burst. I wanted to be strong and to tell her exactly how I felt. Exactly how I felt, so with my fingers clenched so hard I was sure I was bleeding, I said, "I am done with you."

"Olivia," she said. Coming over and trying to hug me.

I said, "Stay away from me."

Dad was right behind me now.

"I'm done with you, too," I said.

Mom said, "Olivia, wait." Maybe she was going to cry. Maybe she wasn't. Who cared?

Dad said, "Calm down."

Delilah said, "Let me get y'all some Cokes."

And like that, I ran out of there and kept on running and never turned back.

CHAPTER 84

Steve Fossett didn't grow up rich. He made his own fortune.

He learned how to swim by diving in the dirty pond on the outskirts of his town.

He swam every day.

He learned how to program computers by being friends with nerds.

He started training his legs for mountain climbing by working in a brickyard.

He read the Scout manual forward and backward and he left his whole stupid family and all the rest of it behind to become the best adventurer in the entire world.

He made his own fortune.

No more sweepstakes for me.

No more waiting on Carlene to go to Monster Jam.

No more Mom.

No more Dad.

I was going to make my own fortune.

I was going to do it on my own.

CHAPTER 85

I ran to my house.

Now Berkeley and Sadie and Jane were over by Melody eating her cookies, which are bribes I'd figured out. Maybe Dad had hired Melody to bribe us. To sit on the porch and look sad and tell us about horseflies. Maybe everyone in this trailer court was in on it. Maybe they were trying to trap us and make us think we could never leave and that our lives were stuck. Maybe the whole thing was a sting operation and Bart was right. I should've been more careful and I should've been on the lookout and my parents were both in on it actually and they were trying to ruin my life and it was working.

"Berkeley!" I said.

She came over. "Melody is going to help with the circus. She said she talked to you about it. She can do the unicycle."

"Berk. I have to go. We have to go."

"Where?"

Where. Where. Where.

"I don't know but I'll take care of you, okay. We'll figure it out."

Berk stared at me.

"Come on. We have to hurry," I said, trying to drag her along.

She pulled away. "We can't leave," she said.

I didn't have time to explain. How could I explain? She wouldn't understand.

"We're going," I said.

She still wouldn't move.

"Dad's back. He's going to take care of us. We can't leave."

"He's not going to take care of us," I said. "He's a jerk and he only cares about himself and he left us, Berk. He left us and Mom."

Her face went white. "He's back," she said, her voice small.

I should have stopped but I didn't. I didn't. I said, "He left us once and he'll leave us again. He doesn't care about us."

She didn't move. Frozen in place. "What about the circus?" she whispered.

The stupid circus. The stupid stupid circus.

"There's not going to be a circus, okay? I made it up. There's no circus. No circus."

She sat on the ground then. Sat there and I couldn't do it. I could not do it.

I went inside. I slammed the door.

Got my bag. Threw in some clothes. Some paper and pens. My notebook. All the rest of the Oreos and a bag of Doritos. The Steve Fossett memoir that I needed to renew at the library and all the money I had in the world which was sixteen dollars and forty-two cents from using the metal detector and which I was saving for Las Vegas in case they needed money for gas and I also grabbed thirty-six Nickle City tickets which could get me candy if I got desperate.

Then I ran back outside.

Berk still sat there and I was sorry but I would figure it out later.

"I'll come back for you," I said. "I promise."

Tears were running down her face and my heart was breaking but I had to go. I had to go.

No more.

And then here they came.

Mom and Dad walking around the corner.

Talking to Delilah.

Taking their sweet time.

The funny thing, Mom was wearing the most beautiful white sundress flowing down to her ankles. Her hair loose and, though she was acting upset, you could tell that now that Dad was back, now that he was walking by her side, she was lit up again.

I wanted to scream.

And Dad, he seemed like he was in charge. A big large and in-charge man.

The two of them almost glowing in the light from the lowering sun.

Barf on a stick.

I turned to find my bike.

"Olivia!" Dad yelled.

I ran faster.

"Olivia!"

I got on the bike, threw my backpack on, and took off for the bike trail.

"Livy!"

He was probably getting his bike. Or maybe just running or maybe he'd stopped to get a latte.

Either way, before either of them could do a thing, I was gone.

I left my sister.

CHAPTER 86

On the bike path there were lots of people.

People laughing.

People jogging.

People holding balloons.

People on Rollerblades.

None of them were running away from home.

None of them had parents who were liars.

None of them lived in Sunny Pines and ate tuna fish sandwiches with Doritos for a living.

Just then, a lady collapsed.

And I gave her CPR.

And everyone cheered.

No I didn't.

I never do anything.

CHAPTER 87

I sat in the park.

Under a pine tree.

I ate Doritos.

I watched police cars go by, with policemen talking on their walkie-talkies.

I met a girl named Persephone who gave me a banana.

I sat there and tried to figure out what to do.

The only thing I could come up with was this: Go to dinner at Bart's house. 911 North Elm Street. Have him take me to FBI headquarters. Save Berkeley.

It was a stupid plan but I wanted to tell the FBI that my parents were lying criminals.

And I wanted to take my first step just like Steve Fossett did. For him it was the fifty miler. For me, it was dinner at Bart's house.

CHAPTER 88

I sat on the grass on the corner of North Elm Street.

In a half hour I was supposed to eat dinner with Bart and his mom and they lived in a little house that had chipped paint and a chain-link fence and the next-door neighbor had four cars on his lawn but still their house was nice. There were flowers in front and a swing and a dog probably.

They probably had cloth napkins.

They probably listened to classical music.

They probably ate kale.

I wondered if Bart would let me stay there until I figured out where to go or what to do.

or . . .

Maybe if they had an extra bedroom I could be a normal part of the family just for a little bit.

I sat.

I wondered what he'd say. I wonder if Bart would think I was brave or strange or stupid.

Just then, a truck pulled up to Bart's house.

A truck. A truck I had seen a million times.

It was Grant.

CHAPTER 89

I thought about getting on my bike and riding away.

Had he followed me? But how?

Was he a part of the search party?

Was there a search party? I hadn't seen any flyers around yet.

What if Bart had lured him there? What if he was about to be SWAT teamed? Was everything about the FBI really true?

I stood up and started walking over even though it wasn't smart. Especially if Grant was out looking for me.

But I was tired.

I got nearer to the house and thought it would be very interesting to see what happens if he was a criminal.

But then, the front door opened.

Bart's mom came out. She was in tight jeans and a tight T-shirt and just like my mom, she had her hair flowing all over the place.

I froze.

"Hey, babe," she said. Surely she wasn't talking to Grant.

Surely.

But then she ran out and before I could even think,

she was jumping into dumb-bum wanted-by-the-FBI, possible criminal mastermind, for-sure-horrible-hygiene Grant's arms.

Just like that.

And then they started kissing.

CHAPTER 90

My heart went down to my stomach.

Bart came out then, too.

He looked horrified.

But not.

He actually looked normal.

Like this kind of thing happened all the time.

He walked past them kissing, turned on the hose, and started watering the flowers.

What was happening?

And then I realized why Bart had been spying on Grant.

He looked across the street at me.

Our eyes locked.

And I couldn't do this anymore.

I couldn't take this anymore.

CHAPTER 91

I turned to run.

Then I didn't turn to run.

I just stood there. In the middle of the road.

He walked over.

He said, "Hey."

I said, "Hey."

He said, "You were missing."

I said, "How did you know?"

He said, "Grant."

We both looked over at them still hugging.

Then I said, "Your mom's boyfriend is Grant?"

And he said, "Yes."

I said, "Oh."

He said, "They fight a lot."

I said, "They do?"

He said, "Yeah."

And I thought about when Grant got mad and me and Bart holding hands and lying there and how scary Grant could get and how Bart's mom loved him because they were kissing even though he got mad and I felt sad for Bart right then.

He said, "Are you okay?"

I looked at him.

Bit my lip.

Then I said, "You turned us in."

"I know."

"Why? Why did you do that?"

He dug his shoe into the pavement. Looked at the ground and said, "I got scared. You sent me that email and when I saw it, I just, I got scared." He paused. Looked at me. "What if something bad happened to you? What if, what if you tried to get a ride with someone or went on the bus and you got murdered. Or you got hurt or lost or you know, something bad?"

My heart beat fast and hard and I felt like I might cry.

"I didn't want to do it but," he said. "But, I just, I wanted you to be okay. I wanted you to have help."

I nodded, the tears welling.

"I could have done it," I said.

And he said, "I know. I know you could've but I just, something inside me, like I can't explain, something in me told me I should call. That it was the right thing to do."

I kept nodding, wiping my eyes.

He kept going. "When I saw you at the pool and I was so worried you would never talk to me again. I was worried and then you came and you were, you were, you were you. Like you just forgave me. I couldn't believe it. There's no one like you, Olivia. No one. Not anywhere."

I wiped my eyes. "What do you mean?"

"What do I mean? I mean you're just so good."

I laughed. "No I'm not."

But he didn't laugh.

He went on. "I have all kinds of crap problems with school and my parents and I'm always grounded and I lied to you. I'm not an FBI agent even though I should be. P.S. I lie about a lot of things and I was getting in all this trouble and when I met you, it was bad. It was so bad. Like I don't have a phone and I'm not allowed on the computer hardly ever and my mom makes me go to aerobics with her. I have to go."

"So it's not for training?"

He shrugged. "It *is* really good exercise. Anyway, everything was so bad and the worst part is Grant. I kept wondering why my mom would date him. He seems so boring and weird."

I laughed. "He mostly is weird."

"I just want my mom to be happy and she's always dating these dumb losers. I just want her to find someone who will love her."

I nodded.

"I didn't think he was good for her and she said I didn't know what I was talking about so then I decided I'd show her. I'd get evidence."

"So you came to Sunny Pines."

"Yep," he said. "And I met you."

I smiled.

"And I found out he is what I thought but also he loves her and also, maybe there's nothing I can do about it."

"Yeah," I said. "Sometimes there's nothing you can do about it."

He laughed. Then he got quiet. "I want to tell you something," he said.

"What?" He looked serious and my heart started up again. What was he going to say?

"I," he paused. "I . . . I made you a pie."

"A pie?"

"I knew you'd come. I knew it. And I wanted to give you something special. So I made it."

I laughed.

Then he said, "I thought we could eat the pie on top of my house and we could watch the sunset and I would say I'm sorry that I lied to you about Grant and I'm sorry that your dad is a butthead and that I'm so glad you're my best friend."

His best friend.

His best friend.

His best friend.

"It's apple brown sugar and caramel on top."

I laughed more now.

And he said, "It's better than McDonald's."

CHAPTER 92

At Bart's house we ate dinner.

We walked to the backyard just as Grant was taking burgers off the grill and when he saw me he said, "Holy crap," and almost dropped the tray.

I said, "Hi." And he said, "Hi? What are you doing here?"

He seemed mad at me, which was weird.

He wanted to know where I'd been.

Bart's mom made us sit down.

"I wasn't gone *that* long," I said.

"You were gone for hours, Olivia. Everyone thought you were just going to cool off but then you didn't come back."

Bart's mom made me a plate. She made one for Grant, too, but he didn't seem to feel like eating. Instead he kept asking me things. Telling me how irresponsible that was.

"I'm going to call your mom right now," he said.

And I said, "Can't we eat?"

He looked at me. "Olivia. She's really upset."

I put down a Dorito. "I know, I know. I let her down."

He stared at me. "You let her down?"

I didn't say anything.

"You didn't let her down. You scared the earwax out of her is what you did."

I ate the Dorito. "She doesn't care."

"She doesn't care? Are you kidding me?" he said. "She's been a wreck. She made your dad leave. Screamed at him."

My heart started thumping. "She did?"

"Oh yeah. It got ugly."

I thought about that. Mom never yelled at Dad. Ever. "Why?"

"He kept telling her to calm down. That it wasn't a big deal and she went ballistic."

My mom. Going ballistic. About me. To my dad.

"And he left?"

"He said he'd find you on his own and took off."

I swallowed. Mom made him leave. She did it.

Then Grant said, "We've all been looking for you."

I looked at the ketchup bottle. "Who?"

"All of us. Me. Bob. Melody. Delilah. Paul. Randy. Jerry. Carlene and Tandi and Lala and Chip. Even Sydney. Baby George. Everyone." He paused for a second. Then he said, "Your whole family."

That's when I really started crying.

CHAPTER 93

I rode to Sunny Pines Trailer Park in Grant's truck.

It smelled like dog and armpit and piña colada thanks to the scent tree hanging from his rearview mirror.

"You nervous?" he asked.

I was watching the houses go by. In every single one, people lived there.

People who talked to each other and fought with each other and ate macaroni and cheese with each other.

People who watched TV and went on bike rides and braided each other's hair.

In every single house there were things that were good and things that were bad. And there were families. All kinds of families that tried their best to hold each other together.

"I'm okay," I said.

When we pulled in, to my surprise, there was a huge WELCOME HOME, OLIVIA sign and an elephant and a helicopter throwing out confetti and a TV camera and forty-five dancers from the hit TV show *So You Think*

You Can Dance doing a modern number about love and reunion and a hundred boxes of Totino's frozen pizzas.

But really, there was Berk in the middle of the street. And Mom. And Melody. And Carlene.

And everyone.

And I ran to Berk and I held her and I said, "I'm so sorry. I'm so so sorry."

She just hugged me and hugged me and hugged me and I hugged her right back.

And then I hugged Mom and she hugged me and she said, "It's going to be okay," and I said, "I know," and then I hugged Melody and Mrs. Sydney Gunnerson and Delilah and Paul and Grant and Carlene and Tandi and Chip and everyone. I hugged everyone because I was home.

CHAPTER 94

On a summer night in the middle of June, the moon big in the sky and the sun, too, Sunny Pines Trailer Park had its first annual CIRCUS UNDER THE STARS FOR-EVER YOURS!!!

Berk made up the name.

There were lights everywhere thanks to Melody and Harry, who was back for now, and a cotton candy machine and a dunking booth that Mrs. Sydney Gunnerson donated the money to rent.

Delilah brought sweet rolls and doughnuts and left-over cupcakes from the bakery.

There was a real live stage that Earl Bowen built and none of us even knew he was a carpenter and even was in the army for ten years and then he lived in Papua New Guinea (!!!!!), he built a real live stage with a curtain and a background that me and Carlene and dumb-bum Bonnie, who thought it was stupid but then did it anyway, the three of us painted and it was actually kind of fun.

There was music and a microphone thanks to Grant and Bob.

Jerry Smith got to bring home some exotic pets from

Petco for everyone to look at, like a bearded dragon, and a gerbil, and a big huge boa constrictor snake.

Berk had a new golden leotard and she and Sadie and Jane did the opening number where they danced and then yelled in their loudest voices:

WELCOME TO THE CIRCUS UNDER THE STARS FOREVER YOURS! PLEASE TURN OFF YOUR PHONES AND ANY OTHER MOBILE DEVICE! WE HOPE YOU ENJOY THE SHOW!!!

And then Bart came out wearing a top hat and his baggy jeans and he made jokes and everyone laughed and he was the Master of Ceremonies.

And soon, the acts started.

Melody rode her unicycle and Paul lifted a couch with three people sitting on it and Carlene and Bonnie performed a lip sync to a One Direction song that wasn't too bad.

Mrs. Sydney Gunnerson did a ventriloquist act with her doll named Agatha and people weren't sure whether to laugh or be serious, but then Mrs. Sydney Gunnerson and her doll named Agatha started laughing so then everyone was laughing.

Randy walked across the stage on his hands and Berk did her tightrope act and only fell twice and I juggled Sprite bottles and sang *Yankee Doodle* at the same time, thank you very much.

And then, this really happened, Grant belly danced! He belly danced wearing these spandex pants and gym shorts over them and no shirt and some sort of mask and me and Bart we could not stop laughing, and Roxi, Bart's mom, kept telling us to shush but she was so red in the face you could tell she was trying not to laugh, too, and Mom was laughing the hardest.

Tandi did a front handspring, which who knew she could do that? Even Carlene had her jaw dropped. I bet she couldn't do that and Chip drove down the street in his truck.

Delilah told a story about a monkey's paw that about made me pee my pants and even the Conways came out and the dad told a few jokes.

The whole neighborhood.

And at the very end, Mom. My mom. She got up and sat on a chair. All by herself with a guitar.

She looked beautiful and small and in her white flowing dress again. The one I thought was for Dad. But maybe it was for her.

She was going to Mountainland Applied Technology at nights. She was seeing a therapist person that we got for free through the government and sometimes we went, too. And she was finally asking people for help.

She got up there and smiled.

"This is for my girls."

And then she started to sing, her voice filling up the night.

No one moved, no one breathed, the notes were so full and real and everywhere, like a dance all their own.

And then, Berk, she crawled up on my lap and the three of us, Mom up there, me and Berk on our lawn chairs, we cried.

And cried.

And cried.

We could do it.

We didn't need luck or seven million dollars or hot-air balloons.

We could do it.

I looked around at everyone sitting there, loving my mom and loving us, too, and I knew it was true.